If the ODs were taking place in a pattern, that meant they weren't random, and that meant...

They stood staring at the map for a few moments, trying to figure out the center. They were all trying to decide just exactly what *was* in that part of town.

Pete was the first to respond. "Oh, my God, it couldn't be."

"What?" several asked.

"Keeping the right proportions and then taking this spiral to its logical end, you come to...well..." He turned to look at Colton. "Don't you live someone right here?" he asked as he put his finger on the map.

"Umm..." said Colton, stepping closer.

"Didn't you buy one of those old brownstones in that area? To fix it up?" one of the officers behind him asked. "Isn't that near you, Colton?"

"Yeah, it is."

"But this doesn't make sense," Marie piped up again. "Why or how could ODs be taking place in a spiral and why closing in on Colton? There's no reason for it. Is there?"

She asked the questions to silence. No one had an answer to either of them.

They all were thinking the same thing. If this really was a pattern they were seeing, then it meant the ODs were no longer random, and they probably were no longer just simple ODs. This meant homicides, and that put everything in a completely different ballpark. And no one really liked to play in that park.

People are dying in the suburbs of Denver, and a young lady from the streets appears to be the latest victim. Thanks to a friend, she doesn't die, but she does display symptoms of drug toxicity from an unknown substance, similar to the other victims. While investigating the deaths, Detective Colton Mitchell notices a change in his teenage daughter, Abby, who can't seem to do without the straws of orange candy her new boyfriend gives her. When Colton takes one of the straws to his friend, Jack, the medical examiner, Jack is brutally slain before he can reveal the source of the substance. Looking at a map with pins of the locations of the crime scenes, Colton realizes that the murders have occurred in a spiral pattern, and the spiral is closing in on his house…

a hard time putting down. *~ Regan Murphy, The Review
Team of Taylor Jones & Regan Murphy*

ACKNOWLEDGMENTS

Special thanks to my editor, Lauri, for wanting my stories; to my editor, Faith, for teaching me so much about writing; to Jack in the art department; and to all the staff at Black Opal Books.

Spiral

Mary Jane Bryan

A Black Opal Books Publication

GENRE: CRIME THRILLER/MYSTERY-DETECTIVE

This is a work of fiction. Names, places, characters and incidents are either the product of the author's imagination or are used fictitiously, and any resemblance to any actual persons, living or dead, businesses, organizations, events or locales is entirely coincidental. All trademarks, service marks, registered trademarks, and registered service marks are the property of their respective owners and are used herein for identification purposes only. The publisher does not have any control over or assume any responsibility for author or third-party websites or their contents.

DEDICATION

*To my husband, Peter Bryan,
for his patience and for
understanding my need
for the computer*

Prelude

In the shadows, a figure leaned against the dark brick of the building. It looked like one of those board cut outs some people have in their yards or leaning against a tree near the street. The only difference was that the board cut outs seemingly have more life in them.

The figure stood motionless, one foot drawn up behind him, his boot on the building. His dark clothes made him blend in with the environment of discolored brick and graffiti.

A man leaning against a building was a common sight.

Even more common were the two figures lying across the sidewalk manhole grate slightly to the right of the figure. These figures were covered from head to toe with ragged blankets.

These two were part of the homeless who spent part of their days panhandling and their nights sleeping on the grates. The openings provided warmth from the steam that came from the city's underground power supply.

This was the inner city.

Downtown.

Doing nothing was a way of life. There were those with little hope for anything better in the future.

The man was here because he understood the cravings and addictions of some of these people. He understood the loneliness, the desperation that characterized so many of them.

He was alone. He was totally removed from his family, with no hope of ever seeing them again. The hatred and resentment that he sensed in so many of these people were also present in him, but many times over. But he believed himself capable of so much more than these people.

He wondered if he had been missed during the time that he had been gone. He sensed that many of these people would never be missed if they disappeared.

That's why they would serve his purpose so well.

He couldn't always control the hatred he felt. Sometimes it would suddenly come upon him, causing wave after wave of feelings, each stronger than the last. When these feelings built to a certain point, the only relief, the only way to make them stop, was to take that hatred and anger out on someone.

It was better because he had learned that these people could be killed, left maimed, or mutilated, if necessary, and no one seemed to care, especially not in this big city, as in other large cities he had watched.

The worst thing he had to cope with was this all-absorbing, all-consuming hatred and anger that had become the controlling factor of his life. Of all the things he could control, he had been unable to stop this.

He had developed a plan of revenge built on this hatred.

So, now he waited patiently.

His patience had already paid off.

His plan was already in motion.

Chapter 1

You hurtin', fair lady?" he asked, in a southern drawl.

"God, yes," she replied. She *was* hurting. If she didn't get a hit soon, she would be in agony. "How much?" she asked. She was not concerned with what he had to offer. Anything would do.

"For you, *fair lady*, it's free today."

"Free? Jeez, you mean it?" She couldn't believe it. One thing she had learned on the street was nothing was free. There was always a price.

"Sure."

He brought his hand out of his pocket. As he held it out to her, he opened it.

She saw several orange pills she didn't recognize. But at this point, she didn't care. As long as they helped, she would take anything. "You sure they're free?" she asked again.

"As I said, just for you, fair lady," was the soft reply.

She glanced up, saw his smile. Maybe he wasn't so bad after all.

But the pain was making everything fuzzy, fast. She saw the smile on his lips but there was none in his eyes. If she had looked longer, she would never have taken the pills. His eyes were as cold as raw steel. In them, she would have seen a pent-up hatred for her and her kind.

She quickly reached out and grabbed the pills. She popped two into her mouth at once, dry swallowing them. She had long since passed the need to have liquid to swallow any pill. She turned and slouched slowly away down the sidewalk. She did not look back. Had she turned, she would not have seen anyone. He was already gone.

She had spotted him down the street. She knew the look of a pusher. If the few dollars in her pocket weren't enough, she would have offered her body.

He saw her coming and knew what she was after. She was skinny to the point of being gaunt. Nurturing herself was the last thing on her mind. She hardly ate. Her focus was on feeding her habit, having enough drugs so she didn't have to think about life.

Life hurt.

A young man playing basketball down the street suddenly stopped, causing the man guarding him to nearly knock him down.

"Damn, man, whaddup?" the man began, but Lon was already off the court. His eyes never left the girl he had spotted down the street. He completely forgot the game as he jogged quickly toward the two people on the corner.

Nancy was already walking away from the man. Lon wondered if she had scored. By the time Lon reached the corner of the building he saw only Nancy down the block. That was not unusual, though. He had not been able to see the other person for the shadows here. Sometimes these people seemed to slip into the woodwork, silently disappearing as soon as their business was done.

He started down the sidewalk after her and watched

her turn and go down to her basement apartment. She had scored! She always went home whenever she was tripping.

He followed her in and gently shut the door. She was totally unaware she had left it open. He liked Nancy. He was her best friend, one of the few she had. He had met her soon after she arrived in town. He felt bad that he had been unsuccessful in keeping her off the streets. He had never made love to her. He was drawn to her for other reasons. Whenever she allowed, he would bring food to her, fix her meals, make sure she ate something.

He watched her carefully. Unless she had been high when she took these pills, they were working quickly. She stood, swaying, in the middle of the room.

Suddenly, she grabbed her throat. She made a gasping, choking sound, doubled over, and held her stomach.

He reached her in two quick strides, catching her as she pitched forward. For a brief moment as she looked at him, recognized him. There was panic in her eyes. It was not panic at seeing him, he could tell, but at some inner realization.

"Bad..." she gurgled. Her eyes rolled back in her head and she started gagging.

His thoughts were frantic. He knew she had been starting to say that she had gotten some bad drugs. Could he get her to throw up those pills? He knew he had to try. He had been with her during many trips, but she had never reacted like this before.

There was a small frig on the counter. He opened it and grabbed a milk carton. He didn't care how long it had been there. He just knew he had to get some down her. Maybe it was spoiled. That would even be better.

He tilted her head back, talking to her constantly. "Drink, Nancy, drink this. You must."

He pushed her head back farther with one hand.

Some milk spilled down onto her neck and checks. He managed to make her swallow about a half cup before she suddenly leaned forward in a massive convulsion of heaving, spasms, and vomit.

He stood behind her, one arm around her, one of her forehead to support her head. When she could not even heave anymore, she collapsed in his arms. She groaned, a low, pitiful sound.

Neither of them had any money, but that wasn't important. He wanted her to get to a hospital. Her lips had a funny color to them and her eyes would not focus. But at least she was breathing, although raggedly.

He left her lying down, on her side, curled in a fetal position, just long enough to run upstairs to ask the neighbors to call Nine-One-One for an ambulance. Then he gathered her in his arms and sat rocking her until the heard the wail of an ambulance siren. For once, it had taken less than the nine-minute average for it to get there. He insisted on going in the ambulance with her.

He was scared. He had known for the longest time that he loved her. In spite of all she did, he was even more convinced now. Seeing her almost die, in such pain, caused him so much anguish, he vowed to get out her out of this place, no matter what the cost.

He had left home and prided himself on not needing his family but if it meant a better life for Nancy, a chance for a life together, he would get on his knees and beg them for help. They could afford it easily.

He couldn't lose her now. His emotions turned to anger. His anger was directed toward the unseen pusher on the corner.

I will find him. Make him pay.

Chapter 2

What a day this has been, Colton thought.
Another OD.
No answers.
Again.
Still.

Abby dropped her purse and several items fell out of it and rolled on the floor just as Colton walked through the kitchen door.

Abby was home? "Hi, honey-bun," Colton said to her, calling her by one of her favorite nicknames he had for her.

She stood up quickly, frowning at him. What a silly thing to call her. Did she used to like that?

"Hi, Dad," she answered, lifting the candy she held to her lips, tilting her head back to put the powdery substance in her mouth.

"Whatcha got there?" he asked. He recognized the straw container but asked anyway.

"Oh, just candy," she replied.

"Share?" he asked.

"Oh, Dad, you know I don't want your germs." She grinned at him. She had been instantly irritated when he first spoke to her. She had almost said something smart to him but stopped herself just in time.

She couldn't stay irritated with him. Here was her favorite person in all the world. At least he had been until Craig came along.

Thinking of Craig made her smile. Her dad mistook it for pleasure at seeing him.

They said only a few words in passing these days. It seemed as if one or the other was gone at any given time. They used to have at least the evening meal together—all three of them—as a family. But no longer. Abby always seemed to be on the go, doing one thing or another.

Why? he wondered. *There has to be a reason. Maybe we could start again. I really miss those family meals.*

"You always said candy was bad for you," he said, teasing her.

"You know, once I got started, it seems I couldn't get enough. But it hasn't put any weight on me. Has it?"

She looked down at herself. She almost seemed pan-icky.

That drew his attention to her figure. He knew these teenage girls were obsessed with looking like stick-figure models. Most men weren't attracted to such thinness, but you couldn't convince teenage girls of that. He was shocked at what he saw. She had lost so much weight. When had that happened?

She was wearing a pair of shorts and a tee shirt. Her young lady's figure had evaporated into "skin and bones."

"Abby!" he exclaimed before he could stop himself.

"What?" she asked, immediately defensive.

"You've lost so much weight. And your hair. What's happened?"

"What do you mean, what's happened? Nothing's happened, Dad. It's fashionable to be thin. Don't you know anything? And since when did you care what I look like? All you care about is that stupid job of yours!"

Her tone was so rebellious, so defensive, so unlike her, that Colton was speechless. Shocked by her attitude, he momentarily had nothing to say.

Never had she questioned the time he gave to his job. She had been proud of his position and what he did. Besides, it wasn't him that passed up dinner. It was her.

By the look of her, she not only missed the meal here at home, she missed it completely.

What did she do that took up so much of her time?

He glanced down at her purse on the counter, lying on its side, the contents sticking out halfway.

There were several "straws" sticking out of it just like the one in her hand. They were orange—*orange?*—striped.

"Are you okay, honey?" he asked. "Something wrong?"

He felt it.

"What could be wrong?" she asked. "Why do you think something's wrong?" She glanced down at the straws sticking out of her purse on the counter and moved quickly to shove them and a couple of other items back into her purse, including the straw she had been eating out of.

Colton was aware of the guilty, furtive movements. These were the very same actions he saw everyday talking to those who had broken the law but were trying to conceal it.

Why would she want to hide candy from him?

Orange?

Something was not right here.

Now, he remembered. "Since when did you start eating orange candy? I thought you hated the taste of oranges. Even the smell of them, or anything made with oranges."

She felt her irritation grow, the urge to snap back at him, to tell him to mind his own business. But she knew if she did, she would possibly be grounded. That just wouldn't do. She had to be with Craig. "Oh, it's just a group thing," she said, smiling at him.

But Colton had seen her emotional response to his question. She had appeared like a spring, ready to snap, and, just as quickly, she had relaxed.

He looked at her, waiting for an answer.

"You see," she began, "it was Craig's idea. He started buying us these candy-filled straws, these stick things, all in different colors, different flavors. He gave me the orange ones. I told him I didn't like orange, but he insisted I try one. He said he liked orange. So, I tried it. Sure enough, it's good." She laughed. "He always has them. And now it seems I can't get enough." She giggled again. "Other kids noticed that we only ate the orange, so they began eating other colors. Now each group has a different color. It's cool."

"Oh," Colton responded. He was relieved. It was just a harmless fad. It would pass. It was nothing. "It's just that you've lost weight, a lot of weight. That's why I thought something was wrong. And you never join your mother and me for dinner anymore. Those times were so special to us as a family."

"There's just so much going on, Dad. I guess I've lost weight because I do miss dinner many times. It's no big deal. Really." She sighed. "I don't think I'll join as many organizations at school next semester. There just are so many meetings, and…"

She stared at him, her eyes pleading with him to understand.

"I understand, Abby. It can get to be too much. Better decide this summer which are most important and stick with a few. By the way, how is the DARE program coming?"

"DARE?" she repeated.

Wow. She had not attended a DARE meeting for the past month. Or had it been two? She couldn't remember. How could she do this? DARE had been so important to her. For some reason, she had forgotten it existed. She had been forgetting a lot of things lately. People expect you to do this or that all the time.

Like forgetting to eat?

"Fine," she responded. "Still hanging in there."

She couldn't remember lying to her dad before.

"Great," he said. "That's my girl. And how's it going with this new boyfriend—or is it?"

He didn't expect her panicky expression at the very mention of him. It was gone in a second's time. If he had not been looking directly at her, he would never have noticed it.

She smiled, shrugging. "Oh, he's as wonderful as ever. I'm so lucky. The other girls are so jealous that he picked me as his girlfriend."

Then her voice lowered ever so slightly, but Colton detected the change.

"But, Dad—" she began.

Just then a horn sounded, interrupting whatever she was about to say to him.

"That's my ride. Gotta go. See ya, Dad."

He opened his mouth to ask who or where, but she was gone so quickly, the storm door banging shut behind her. As he stood there unable to move, the car roared away.

He not only felt, but knew, he had just missed something important. What had she started to say?

He noticed one of the candy sticks on the floor. She

had gathered things back into her bag so quickly she had missed this one that had rolled under the edge of the cabinet next to the cabinet wall.

Chapter 3

Colton absent-mindedly reached down and picked up the candy straw stick. He walked around the counter, pulled open their junk drawer, and shoved it in along the left side toward the back among some pencils and pens.

He jumped when the phone rang but only because it was so close to him, to his head, but because his inner thoughts were still attuned to Abby. He reached out and quickly grabbed the receiver.

"Mitchell," he said into the phone, probably more brusquely than he intended.

"Mr. Mitchell?" a voice asked.

He had heard the voice before, but not recently. He couldn't place it.

"Yes," he repeated.

Obviously, Colton thought. He still wasn't in the best of moods this morning.

"Mr. Mitchell, we don't usually call like this and really can't all the time, not on an individual basis, I mean, but..." The voice hesitated, trailing off. Colton was rapidly getting a strange feeling, a bad feeling, and was about to ask who this was, then the voice continued.

"Oh, I'm sorry. This is Paul Myers, the vice-principal at Middleton School."

Middleton Preparatory School was the private school Abby attended. It was not far from their home.

"Oh, yes, Paul, how are you?" Colton responded.

Although the bad feeling was still with him, threatening to settle in, he figured Myers was calling about some bazaar or other fund-raising event for the school. Even though it was a private school, the administration did allow projects to help the parents get involved with their children's education and bring in special programs on occasion.

The bad feeling was about Abby. That much he could identify. Believing Abby to be an outstanding, exceptional student, however, he wasn't connecting the feeling with a call from the school.

"Mr. Mitchell, I'm not sure how to begin this, but I suppose I might as well just plunge in, right?"

The feeling gave him a jab, almost like a physical blow to the ribs.

"Abby?" he asked Myers.

"Oh, you already know, then," Myers responded. Colton heard the relief in the man's voice.

"Know what?" Colton asked.

"You don't know?" Myers asked, his voice deflated again.

Colton felt as if he were in a scene from Laurel and Hardy or one of the old slapstick routines he caught on TV every once in a while when he just wanted to relax and let his brain go brain-dead, usually after an exceptionally hard day at the office.

"Paul, could you get to the point, please?" Colton urged in his most professional voice. This voice always told people to quit messing around and get it over with.

It had the right effect on Myers. "As you know…

uh…Abby has always been one of our most outstanding students…uh…straight As, cheerleader, member of several clubs…uh…and just as important as that, she's always been a respectful, nice young lady. Very polite."

Myers paused again.

"Yes, that sounds like Abby," Colton agreed.

Why was the feeling increasing, just sitting there in the pit of his stomach, going around and around? Why had he detected an unspoken "But" at the end of Myers' spiel?

"Well, lately, she's been…well…less, let's say… than her usual self."

"Less?" repeated Colton. What a strange way to describe something or someone. "Less? What is that supposed to mean?"

"Well, maybe that wasn't exactly the right word to use, but it did come to mind. Well, you see, she's been less…diligent, shall we say…in her school endeavors."

Colton knew Myers still wasn't saying what he really wanted to say. "Paul, we're both adults here. Would you please just come right out and say what you mean, what you need to?" Colton asked, finding himself growing impatient with the man.

"Okay, okay," the man agreed, but Colton still felt the hesitation. This was going to be something about Abby he did not want to hear, he knew that now, but he needed to know.

The feeling hit him again. Hard.

The vice-principal was still talking, "…Abby's grades have fallen during the past month, enough that all, and I do mean all, of her teachers are concerned. It's okay, sometimes, for one grade to slip a little with an exceptional student, it may only indicate a lack of interest in that particular subject, and it passes, but this…this is overall. She's been missing cheerleading practice, even football games. She hasn't been to a DARE meeting all month—" Myers said as quickly as he could, as if he wanted to get it all out as soon as possible.

"What?" Colton interrupted, almost shouting into the receiver. "Are you sure you have the right student?" he asked, but the feeling had already told him Myers had the right student.

"Sorry—"

"Thanks for calling, Paul. I'll handle it."

The man hung up with obvious relief.

ତ∕ଚତ∕ଚ

Colton stood still for several minutes, numbed by the facts he had just learned. He realized he was leaning his head against the door facing. He couldn't think. He didn't want to think. He certainly didn't want to face the fact that Abby had some sort of problem.

His problem was that he immediately thought of her abusing drugs.

But, wait. Maybe that wasn't the problem at all. Just because she was having some trouble at school, had changed her normal habits, didn't necessarily mean she was on drugs. He had never been a parent that jumped to conclusions or went to extremes with his discipline of Abby.

He realized he immediately thought of drugs because that's what he dealt with most of the time. But was that really all? At the point of Abby's hesitation and when talking with the vice principal, didn't the color orange flash before him? What did the color orange have to do with Abby?

The only thing she had ever touched that was orange was that candy she had earlier.

Colton's head jerked up.

The straw.

Could it be that obvious? Surely not, he thought.

He took three long strides across the kitchen, yanked open the drawer where he had put the straw.

Pulling it out, he looked at it, brought it to his nose, and smelled it. It smelled like an orange. It was a full straw.

Good. He would take it to Jack, let him analyze it.

Colton was sure his friend would prove him wrong. The straw would simply contain candy, that's all. Nothing threatening, nothing bad.

He was sure a good talk with Abby would take care of the problem at school.

Didn't you just try to talk with her? a nagging voice asked him.

He stuck the straw in his pocket. He had to interview the young lady who had recently OD'd.

Chapter 4

"Sir?" Colton asked.

He was at the hospital with Pete. They had gone to question this latest overdose case. Pete was Colton's partner on the police force.

Lon felt a hand on his shoulder as the voice spoke. He turned around and looked up into the face of what he instinctively knew was a cop. The cop's partner, Pete, stood beside him. "I understand you're with the young lady who was brought in a short time ago."

"Yes, sir," Lon agreed. He leaned back in his chair, looked up at Colton. He had been bent over, his elbows on his knees, his head in his hands. He had not been told anything yet about Nancy's condition. "How is she?" he asked.

"As far as I can understand, she's going to pull through," Colton told him.

The young man relaxed. He leaned back in his chair, shut his eyes. He sighed.

"But I'm not the doctor," Colton continued, "so you'll have to hear it from him."

Lon raised his head again, looking at Colton. He nodded.

"I'm a detective. Homicide," Colton continued. "Are you a relative?"

"No, sir," Lon replied. "I'm a good friend. Actually, I—I love her," he said. "The boyfriend, I guess you could say."

His eyes filled with tears which threatened to fall. He didn't care. That was the first time he had said that to anyone, had admitted his feelings out loud. He had never even told Nancy. Yet it seemed important to let this man know who he was, how he felt about Nancy.

"Do you know any of her relatives, anyone we could talk to about her condition? I understand you were with her when the ambulance came?"

"Yes, sir," Lon agreed. "I was with her when she got sick. As soon as I could leave her for a few seconds, I ran upstairs and asked them to call the ambulance."

"Stay here," Colton commanded. He walked over to the nurses' station.

Stay here? Lon asked himself. *Stay here? Where does the cop think I'm going to go?* He wasn't going anywhere until he found out about Nancy, heard for himself that she was doing okay. Besides, the partner had only taken a few steps away.

Stay here? He almost laughed at the thought, but given the gravity of the situation, he knew the cops would never understand just what struck him as funny.

Colton returned.

"Her name's Nancy Wilson?" he asked Lon.

Lon nodded in consent.

"Have you ever known her by any other names?" Colton asked.

"No, just Nancy," came the reply.

What was the cop getting at?

"Do you know any of her relatives, anyone we can contact about her?" he repeated.

"No," Lon answered again. "But…"

Colton waited patiently. "But what?" he finally asked, when it seemed the young man may not continue. People in situations like this usually started to say things that were important then changed their minds, wondering if they were telling too much.

Lon shrugged. "It's just that…I probably know her as well as anyone, or as well as anyone here in Denver. I met her when she first came here."

"Do you know where she's from?" Colton asked.

Lon shook his head then stopped. "Wait," he said, snapping his fingers. "Think," he said to himself, out loud. "I got it. I remember. The bus she came in on at the time was from St. Louis. I not only saw it, but I heard a couple of people talking about how cold it was here compared to St. Louis and why hadn't they brought a coat. Yeah, St. Louis, that's it," he repeated. "She was young. It was several years ago. I tried to keep her off the streets. I wanted her to stay with me, but it's hard, you know. The pimps have ears, you know?"

Colton understood what he was saying. The pimps certainly did have ways of keeping control over their "ladies." Drugs were a major way. That and fear. Even the love of this young man wouldn't have been enough to hold her or make her defy her pimp.

Lon seemed pleased with himself that he had been able to remember.

Colton knew, though, that the pimp would know that Nancy had left his territory in an ambulance. You better believe the pimp would not be anywhere near to claim any knowledge of her.

Colton started to ask him what he had been doing hanging around the bus depot but knew that wasn't important right now.

This girl was important to Colton, and he was going

to find out all he could about her. She displayed all the symptoms the other victims had. The big difference was this girl was still alive. All indications showed she would probably pull through. And it was only by the efforts of this young man that she was alive. That meant he had gotten to her within minutes, maybe even seconds, of her having taken the drugs.

Recently, seven homeless persons had been killed around the Denver area. All seven had displayed some of the same symptoms, although Jack, the medical examiner, had not been able to pinpoint the connection between them.

Colton felt sure this man knew something. He held an important clue. The problem was, the young man probably didn't know or realize he knew anything. That's where Colton came in. He had to ask enough and the right questions to get the answers he wanted.

Lon wasn't being hostile to them, as so many were from this part of the city, but Colton realized Lon had immediately recognized them for what they were.

No, Lon wasn't being rebellious. But neither would he volunteer any information. That was, unless Colton could convince him of the relevance and *importance* of Nancy. Chances were, he wasn't even aware of the other deaths.

To Colton, Lon didn't look like the usual user himself but neither did he look like someone who sat around watching CNN or C-Span all the time, either. These people didn't spend any of their money on a local newspaper. He knew his way around the street. That's why he knew something.

"You use, Lon?" he asked, suddenly.

"Oh, no, sir," Lon said, quickly. He sat up straighter. "I never have."

"Is that a fact?" Pete asked, entering the conversation

for the first time. Pete's tone told the young man he didn't believe him.

Colton shot Pete a warning glance. Lon was not hostile so far. His greatest concern obviously was Nancy. But Colton didn't want to offend him, or they would get nothing else out of him. Pete should know better than to say things like that. "But Nancy did?" Colton asked.

Lon just nodded. He had a drawn, worried look on his face. Colton saw the face of an old young man. "I tried to get her to stop, lots of times. It's hard, you know."

Colton nodded. He knew. He dealt with druggies every day.

"Once she started, she kept on because—" Lon stopped again.

Colton waited, raising his eyebrow.

"Well...because she couldn't stand being a prostitute, not deep down. She hated herself for it, and the drugs made her forget. You know?"

Lon was in danger of crying.

Colton reached out and patted his shoulder. "You'll still have to get this from the doctor, of course, but it's my understanding that Nancy came pretty close to death."

Lon nodded. He had been there.

"The doctor would like for her to be able to be released into the custody of someone who cares for her. She will need lots of attention after this. She doesn't need to be on the streets. Chances are, by the time she physically gets over this, she'll be withdrawn. That's if, and that's a really big if, she has constant care. Is there any way that can be arranged?"

Lon looked up at Colton and nodded. He looked at Pete then back at Colton. "There must be something here I'm missing," he began. He remembered he was talking to cops. *Homicide* cops.

"Why do you say that?" Colton asked quickly. He wanted to keep Lon talking. He sensed him starting to withdraw.

"Well, Nancy's just another street girl to you guys, isn't she? So, who cares, right? There are thousands like her out there in this city. Some come in to get their stomachs pumped or to have abortions or for other reasons. At least, I mean they come here to University Hospital. So, what I'm getting at is this. Why are you guys here now? What's so special about Nancy? She just OD'd on bad drugs. Didn't she?"

As Colton suspected, this young man was smarter than the usual ones they met off the streets. "I'll tell you why we're here if you'll first tell me who you are," Colton offered.

He pulled up a chair and sat down.

That was the cue for Pete to disappear. He did, casually strolling down the hall to the nurses' station. Pete didn't mind. He was a bachelor, and he had spotted a couple of really cute nurses when they first came in.

Often, a person was willing to talk with just one of the policemen. It would be the one that the person has perceived as the one he or she had judged as being receptive and most sympathetic to them. Colton knew Lon had chosen him, probably even before Pete's remark about the drugs. Lon would not have been aware of this unconscious choice. It was just something a policeman or policewoman could pick up on after being on the force for a while and being in on so many cases.

All situations were different, yet at the same time, all were alike. It was a funny truth, but one that had to be accepted as part of the nature of the job.

"My name's Lon Jones," he began. At least the first name was correct. "I'm just someone who loves and wants to care for Nancy. Has Nancy done something wrong? Is that why you're here? Besides using, that is."

Colton decided not to pursue the young man's name right now. "Only possession, but we'll skip that for now. Look," he said, leaning closer to Lon. It was an old trick, intended to take the person into your confidence. It made the person feel special. "Are you willing to help us with something?"

Lon wasn't sure. He said nothing for several long seconds. "That all depends. What is it?" he asked.

"Nancy's reaction to these drugs is the same as several cases that have come to our attention lately. The only difference is that Nancy is the only one still alive. The others are stretched out on cold slabs in the morgue. I suspect the only reason she's alive is because you were right there with her when she started flipping out. And that brings me to an important point here." Colton paused. He was watching Lon closely. He knew when someone was lying. The only lie he suspected so far was the last name, and that could be dealt with later. But who knew? Jones could really be his last name. "Did you see the person Nancy bought the drugs from?"

"No, I didn't," Lon said, looking straight at Colton.

"But you were just seconds behind her. Why didn't you see him? Or her?"

"Well, because of the angle of the building where she was, and I was. She was here." Lon held his hands up, indicating a point. "And I was here." Another point in the air. "The corner of the building kept me from seeing whoever it was. The only person I saw was Nancy, talking with someone, then reaching out, taking something from someone. I knew what was happening. That's when I left the game and started after her. Her apartment was halfway down that block. I figured that's where she was headed. Even if she beat me there, I have a key."

"Okay," Colton said. "So how long do you think it

took you to get from the basketball court to the corner?"

Lon shrugged. "Fifteen seconds, maybe, I don't know. I was jogging pretty fast."

"Okay. So, when you went around the corner, who else did you see and where were they?"

Lon frowned, trying to remember. He shook his head. "Nobody," he said. "Well, nobody but Nancy, of course. Well, nobody on that side of the street, anyway."

"And the other side?" Colton prompted.

"Just two guys sitting on the steps of an apartment. But they live there. They're out on the steps all the time. I may even have waved to them like I always do, I really don't remember. But they belong there."

"Are you sure there was no one else?" asked Colton again. "What about the pusher?"

Lon frowned again. He seemed genuinely puzzled, trying to think about it. "No, there was no one there. I'm sure."

"But you said it was only seconds before you reached the corner. Was the person already crossing the street, on the other side, or what?"

"Honest," Lon said. "There was no one there."

"Lon, are you holding out on me?"

"Oh, no, really. You know as well as I do that if those guys don't want to be seen, they aren't." Lon looked Colton straight in the eye. He knew Colton couldn't deny it. Lon rubbed his temples. "Sorry, nothing else. Maybe those two guys will remember something, if you can get them to talk."

"I may not get them to. But what about you? Will they talk to you?"

"Hey, man, don't do that to me."

Colton knew what he was saying. To show up with a cop, asking questions, would certainly give you a name on the street. Your life wouldn't be worth much.

"Let me find out my own way, okay? No cops. They wouldn't talk then, anyway."

"I know," agreed Colton. "Let me know, okay?" he continued as he stood up. "And, Lon?"

Lon looked at him.

"I really hope Nancy gets over this okay."

"Thanks, man," Lon said.

Chapter 5

As the car sped away, Abby grew quiet, although Craig was chatting away.

She knew things had changed, and she still had just enough of her own will to realize it and worry about it. But only just a little. Most of the time now when someone mentioned homework or asked if Abby would help them, she just blew it off with a laugh.

In short, most of the time, she just didn't care about anything anymore.

She pulled one of the orange-striped straws out of her purse and practically emptied the whole contents into her mouth. It tasted so good. She always wanted some of this candy. She just couldn't get enough. If she thought she didn't have any, she almost panicked. A quick glance in her purse reassured her each time that she had plenty.

She never felt hungry anymore, for any real food. This candy seemed to fill her physical needs. Yet, deep down the nagging thought was there that all this weight she was losing was dangerous to her health, especially at the rapid rate she was losing it. Her clothes were beginning to hang on her.

Now even her dad had noticed.

Starting the fad of each group having a certain color of candy had seemed a cool thing at first, and people were still into it. But no seemed to be eating as much candy as she did. And she ate so much because Craig bought it for her.

At this point, she looked over at Craig, who pointed at the glove box, laughing.

But it was not a good laugh and, when she first glanced at him, it seemed her heart had skipped a beat. This time it was not because she thought he was so good looking. In fact, he had looked like a picture of a demon she had seen in a book. She had blinked, and the impression was gone as he had turned toward her. Boy, was she getting weird lately.

Demons!

But she didn't like the feeling it left her with.

ᘒᘒ

At first, Craig had seemed so cool, and Abby had enjoyed the jealousy of all the other girls.

"Abby!"

The voice she had hoped to hear called to her softly, causing her to turn from her locker.

"Hi," she breathed, smiling. Her heart started beating faster.

"How's it going, lady?" the young man asked, reaching out to touch Abby's arm, managing to make the touch a caress.

"Oh, fine. Just great. You?"

How dumb, thought Abby. *Can't you think of anything more interesting to say? Fine. What kind of a word is that? He might be attracted to you now, but if you keep up dumb comments like that, he'll very soon be bored and dump you.*

Abby still couldn't believe that Craig, the new boy in school, had singled her out and just within a day or two of his enrolling here at Middleton. She knew she was pretty and witty—usually—but so were several other girls in her class. Talk about luck.

She closed her locker and turned to him, positioning herself so that their bodies were very close, just an inch away from touching. He had placed one hand on the locker above her and leaned in toward her.

"You going to Rick's tonight?" he asked.

Rick was giving a party.

"Sure. Always," she responded with a smile. She wondered if he could hear, or even see, her heart beating so fast. She had read plenty of the little fluff romance novels that talked about some man or another as a "heartthrob," and now she understood what it meant. Her heart was actually beating faster.

"Great. I'll see you there, then, okay?" Craig said, returning her smile with one of his own. He gave her a wink.

"Sure. I'm usually there around eightish," she said.

"Cool. See ya."

Craig reached out and touched her arm, causing her to have goosies up and down her arms.

His approach to her had been the appropriate one. He seemed to already know how the program worked. He had probably already asked and knew she liked to get to know a guy a little bit before going out with someone on an individual basis. Meeting at a party first was more her style.

He was a little older than Abby, a senior, too. He had his own car, a red Camaro. At least she thought she had seen him drive away from school yesterday in a red Camaro.

No one else had seen him. She had gotten to school

early this morning to watch for him, even calling Sarah the night before to meet her early. They were disappointed, though. They watched the student parking lot and waited for him to appear until they very last minute before they had to make a mad dash to homeroom.

They slid into their seats just as the last bell rang.

Abby had looked at Sarah and shrugged. If Craig was late after just three days at a new school, it certainly wouldn't endear him to the teachers. Yet, they seemed to already be partial to him. He just had a certain quality about him, he was so likeable.

She watched him now until he disappeared into the crowd of students in the hall, watched as he greeted first one student, then another. How did he know so many so soon? She turned the opposite way, toward her next class. She couldn't wait to tell Sarah and the others. They would just die.

Of course, they would be at Rick's tonight, too, but they all knew this meant he would "be" with Abby. They couldn't talk about anything else for the rest of the day. Abby certainly couldn't keep her mind on her classes for thinking of him.

The day seemed to float by.

Several of them looked and hung around the parking lot after school, but no red Camaro pulled away. Abby agreed with the rest that it must have been someone else, maybe just a visitor to the school.

But she had been so sure it was him.

෴

Craig really impressed them Friday night, even the young men of the group, when he convinced them he never used drugs, not even occasionally. That attitude put him in solid with their crowd.

Craig and Abby started going together.

Now, Abby wasn't sure what had come over her lately.

Whereas before her cheerleading, DARE activities, and homework had been priorities, especially homework, she now found her thoughts, her very world, centered on Craig and what he wanted to do, where he wanted to go.

And it seemed they went somewhere every day after school for a couple of hours.

No matter where they went, however, he always pulled up in front of her house a few minutes before five o'clock, giving her time to get inside, change and be settled with her homework before her mom and dad came home from work.

Since she was always here, at home, smiling as always, when her mom got home, neither Marsha nor Colton had reason to think anything had changed in her life.

But Abby knew things had changed, yet she seemed unable to pinpoint just what or how. The strange thing was, she just didn't seem to care anymore.

A short time ago, she would never have dared not to turn in her homework assignments. She certainly would not have missed cheerleading practice for anything.

But there she was last night, embarrassing herself in front of everyone at the football game because she had to fumble through a cheer, literally following everyone else, which put her a movement behind all the time. Once there was a new routine, just learned that week, but she still didn't know it.

As late as Thursday, the squad captain had warned her about coming to practice and learning the new routine. Abby was a fast learner, and, even at that late date, she would have picked up the motions, but she had not shown up for practice after school. The other girls were really concerned because Abby had never missed a practice. She also always added a certain spark to the squad. They felt her absence. But it didn't just affect the new routine. There were several cheers where the girls paired off, needing each other. They did these cheers every game, part of their standard program. Abby's partner had to sit these out, cheering and clapping at the side of the squad. She was so angry at Abby and let everyone know how she felt.

A boyfriend was one thing. They all understood that, and they were still quite envious of her getting Craig, but they all agreed that he was demanding too much of her time, that he could come and watch practice, then drive her home. But they hadn't been able to convince Abby to stand up to him and insist he do it her way. Instead, she was just following him in all things.

Her teachers had already pulled her aside, at first concerned that maybe something had happened at home, wanting to give her the benefit of the doubt and give her a chance to make up her homework. They were willing to do this because it was so unusual for Abby.

But after a couple of weeks of hit-and-miss assignments being turned in, and those not up to her usual standards, they were all concerned. It was so out of character for her that she became the topic of conversation at several lunch hours in the teachers' lounge.

Craig was mentioned, but they had noticed her with boyfriends before, so that relationship was dismissed as minor. The teachers had been around long enough to recognize such things as "puppy love" and felt it would pass, just as previous ones had.

They promised to start recording all her unusual behavior. No, they agreed they didn't and probably wouldn't do this for some students, not just anybody, but they also agreed that Abby was special to them all. They didn't want to see a potential problem go beyond help.

Chapter 6

To Abby's credit, she had tried to break it off with Craig once when they had only been going together two weeks. When she tried buying the straw candy sticks from the store with her friends, it had not tasted the same to her as the ones Craig had always give her. When she mentioned it to Sarah, Sarah had tasted Abby's, the one from the store. Sarah had just shaken her head, laughing at Abby, saying her taster must be off that day. It had tasted just like Sarah's always had. So, she had gone to Craig for some of his. He had promised to give her some only if she came back to him, only if she promised to be a "good" girl and do what she was told.

He had said it in such a way she thought he was just kidding, but now she knew better. He didn't seem willing to let her go. There was almost an underlying, unspoken threat in the air, a threat that if she tried to break up with him again, something dreadful would happen to her or to her family.

She knew this for sure, yet didn't know how she knew.

Abby had forgotten what her dad had said about her seeming to have some special abilities. She had forgotten that he had urged her to follow her "feelings" to help her make the right decisions about people.

She knew there was something about Craig that wasn't quite right, but she just couldn't leave.

She was afraid to.

She was even more afraid to tell anyone, even her dad, how she felt.

Riding in Craig's car with the wind blowing in her hair, Abby tried to think. She frowned in thought, an expression that was not lost on Craig.

Abby was trying to picture a time when Craig had given, or even offered, the orange candy from his supply to anyone else. She could not remember him ever doing so, even to Sarah, who at first always seemed to be with them.

Did he put something in hers to change it?

Craig laughed, reaching over to pat her hand, bringing her from her own thoughts to turn to look at him.

"You know, it's a good thing you can't become addicted to this kind of candy or you'd be in trouble."

His voice was light, teasing, and she relaxed, dropping her worry that she was growing dependent on having this candy.

He was right. A person didn't grow addicted like this. After all, it was only colored sugar.

Wasn't it?

She laughed in response to him, throwing her head back in the wind, turning her head to look at him. She caught her breath, jerking upright in her seat, forcing herself to look straight ahead.

The look that passed across Craig's face was fleeting, so quickly gone that Abby wondered if she had imagined it.

Yet the look had been real enough to cause her heart to jump, miss a bet, and now was beating hard.

Dad! Dad! Help me! Help me, please!

ひろん

He knew he couldn't always control the hatred he felt. Sometimes it suddenly came upon him, causing wave after wave of strong feelings, each stronger than the last. When these feelings built to a certain point, the only relief, the only way to make them stop, was to take that hatred and anger out on someone.

He always felt it coming. It started first as a tingling in his muscles.

For the first couple of attacks, the surges of feeling had so incapacitated him, had left him so weak for so long, that he could not even move.

But he had learned to control himself.

He knew this was one time he needed to calm down.

Chapter 7

Abby!

Although Colton had been thinking about her, he thought he heard her call to him. He automatically looked up to her room, yet he knew she had just left in a car with this new boyfriend of hers.

But her voice had called to him, so clearly, so distinctly, that she could easily have been in the same room with him.

She needed him.

Somehow, in some way, for some reason, she needed him. He felt that for sure. There was no doubt in his mind.

But what was wrong?

Her weight was wrong, that was true. He knew the stylish, the fashionable thing with teenagers now or even society in general, was to be pencil thin. For some reason, young ladies seemed to think this was beautiful, especially in their bikini bathing suits in the summer.

He wished he could convince her that most men liked a little "meat" on their bones. Holding and making love to a skeleton wasn't the ideal situation for most men.

But women couldn't be convinced!

So, he didn't consider the weight the primary problem. Abby would get over that.

What next? His mind started ticking off all the areas he thought might be a problem for her.

School?

Classwork?

Oh, surely not, he thought. Abby had one of those minds that made learning easy. She seemed to hardly ever study. Certainly, she never stressed over it, yet she made practically all A's on her progress reports.

Whatever happened to calling them report cards, he wondered. He smiled to himself. Progress in the form of a progress report for school. He remembered one time she made a "B" in history just at the mid-point of the semester, and that did stress her. She didn't even want to show them the report that time.

They had a long talk at that time about over-achievers, which could be just as bad as under-achievers. Each condition was a symptom of a deeper, inner problem.

Abby had relaxed.

So, it couldn't be school as the problem, simply because the teachers, at least one of them, would have called by now, concerned with Abby. Most of the teachers at her high school seemed to be conscientious, dedicated educators. He and Marsha made a point of meeting all their daughter's teachers. They made a point of attending all the parent-teacher conferences. All Abby's teachers had nothing but genuine praise and liking for her.

No, it couldn't be that, or he would know. *Why didn't he know*? A small voice interjected.

Thrown off guard by the thought, Colton blinked. Yes, why couldn't he tell what was wrong with her? The thought caused him to frown.

The boyfriend? Could it be something about the new boy in school? She had smiled when he asked about him, but wait—

Colton closed his eyes, picturing Abby standing there a few minutes ago.

Yes, there it was. For a split second, a fleeting moment only, when he asked about the boy, Abby's face had registered an expression, unreadable, but immediately changed to a smiley face.

But there was something.

Colton forced himself to relax, leaning back once again on the counter. This was his technique when he wanted to really concentrate on something. He was usually able to recall what he needed, then to feel it.

With his eyes still closed, he saw Abby, looked at her with different eyes, for a different reason than before.

He gasped.

He no longer saw his beautiful daughter of just a few weeks ago. He saw a guilty, furtive expression on her face, especially when she glanced at the candy straws.

Now, here was what he wanted, the expression when he asked about the new boyfriend.

Could it be? He knew what he saw, but he almost refused to accept it. He had to admit it, though, because it had been there.

Fear.

That's what he saw for an instant of time in Abby's eyes when Craig's name was mentioned.

Pure, unadulterated fear.

What could Abby be afraid of from a young man she had known only a few short weeks? Or, how long? Abby was such a strong-willed person. Could he have intimidated her somehow already?

Something was there, evidenced in the cry for help he just heard from her, felt from her.

He needed to find her.

With his eyes still closed, he thought about the first time he discovered he even had a daughter…

∽∾∽

Six years earlier:

He had traveled back to his hometown on what he thought was just a nostalgic trip, but it soon became something else. An elderly man he remembered from his childhood was still sitting in the same place in the old general store that he had been when Colton was just a kid growing up in this small town.

Midland.

Midland, Arkansas.

Population 825.

Yes, Colton remembered him. He seemed old when Colton was a boy; yet, here he was, still looking old, even older if that were possible.

"Come back because Marsha Miller's little girl's missing, have you? Poor little Abby. Still, she hain't been the first, and she won't be the last."

The old man looked at Colton sharply, his eyes clear, questioning.

But Colton wasn't paying attention to the look the old man was giving him.

Marsha had a daughter! Marsha Miller had been Colton's girlfriend in high school. They had been inseparable until Colton had gone away to college and Marsha went to California to live with an aunt. He had written her many letters, but there had been no response. Then, a final one came from her, asking him to stop writing. He had, with a broken heart.

And he didn't know she had a little girl.

Colton knew where he was heading. He was going to

the home where Marsha had lived twelve years ago. He had practically lived at it while they were going steady.

Had it been twelve years?

So long?

As he drove along, his memories of her were strong. They had been a really "hot" item the last two years of high school. Everyone had called them the "M and M's" because their names were so much alike. Not only their names, but they got along so well. They had broken the relationship when he announced that he was going away to college. Sure, Marsha had cried when he left, that was expected, but, as the remembered, not a whole lot.

In fact, his ego had almost been hurt by the way she carried on so little!

But the important thing now was to locate her, and find out if her daughter really was missing. He needed to get the facts.

As he had rounded the last corner to her house, his brain registered how this street, these houses, had not changed at all, except for a little TLC, of course.

Yes, the name on the mailbox was the same, and still in need of repainting.

Colton had parked his car on the street, about half-way down from the house. If the mailbox had not had the name on it, Colton would still have suspected he was at the right place because of the number of cars around it. He had pulled up behind two other cars on the street.

He rang the doorbell, and it struck him that he had not even thought about what he was going to say to Marsha. Before he had time to think about it, though, the screen door opened, and she stepped out.

Colton caught his breath! Here was the same Marsha he had left twelve years ago. Here was the same flaming red, gorgeous hair, cut now in a modern style. She was still slim and beautiful, hardly looking a day older, even with her red-rimmed eyes and tear-stained cheeks.

"Colton!" she breathed. She was in his arms before he knew it. Colton felt as if he had come home at last. She felt so right and wonderful in his arms. The last twelve years may never have been, the way he felt holding her, stroking her hair with one hand and her back with the other, as she used to.

She started sobbing.

"Shh," Colton said, breathing in the scent of her hair, almost swaying with the thrill of the touch and smell of her. He remembered thinking, *This is why I haven't married all these years. I've never stopped loving her.*

"Shh, it's all right, please don't cry," he had begged her. This was a different cry from when they parted long ago. This was a heart-wrenching cry that had nothing to do with him or his ego. In this cry was all the anguish of the knowledge of a daughter not returning home.

He had held her for several long minutes, until she quieted down, and backed away from him.

"Oh, Colton, how good to see you." She sighed. "But why are you here? You couldn't possibly know about Abby missing? We've been trying to keep it as quiet as possible."

"I didn't know when I first got into town this morning," he said. "My trip was simply nostalgic. One of those 'back to the old hometown roots' sort of thing. I just had a sudden urge awhile back to come here, to see the old place again. I ran into Old Man Ogden at the mercantile, and he recognized me. He asked if I'd come to town because of your daughter."

He frowned. "Marsha, I'm sorry, but I didn't even know you had a daughter. When did you marry? Tell me what's been happening."

She had stopped sobbing and had stepped away from him, and now she looked down, twisting her handkerchief around in her hands. "Shall we go back twelve years?" she asked.

"Sure," he replied. "It's always good to start at the beginning."

He smiled, hoping to cheer her up, but she remained solemn.

"Let's sit on the swing," she said, turning toward the end of the porch.

Amazing, thought Colton. *This is the same porch swing we sat in then. It has the same narrow, green boards, the same rusty chain holding it to the ceiling. Wow, even the same squeaks as we sat down.*

Colton took her hands in his.

"When you left to go to college," she began, "I left to go live with my Aunt in California."

Colton nodded. That much he knew.

"She was wonderful in taking care of Abby. Auntie and Uncle had never had any children of their own, so they literally doted on her, on us, really. Uncle made enough that my Aunt stayed home, and she took care of Abby while I worked.

"Auntie never asked me to pay rent or buy groceries, but she felt it was good for me to work to provide for Abby's needs. Fortunately, I found a job that paid a good salary and had good benefits. We only moved back here about a year ago when Mom had a stroke. Dad was killed five years ago in a car accident in Fort Smith, and Mom's always had high blood pressure. Auntie said she'd help us with finances if we needed her."

Here, Marsha flashed a smile, which made Colton's heart skip a beat. That beautiful smile! But now it was only a fleeting one.

"Everyone should have an aunt like my Auntie Jane," she said.

"But your husband? Your marriage? What about

them? When did you marry?" Colton asked.

She looked straight at him. "I've never been married," she whispered.

"But…your little girl…Abby—" he began. "Wait! Just how old is Abby?"

"Twelve."

"Twelve!" Colton exclaimed. "Twelve! When— When was she born?"

"February 11, 1965," Marsha replied. "That's why I went to live with Auntie in California, to have my baby. And Auntie never blamed me, or judged me, or 'preached' at me. She just simply took me in and loved me. She and Mom had been as close as sisters could be, and she would have done anything for her, and for me. There was never any question about giving up the baby up. No matter what, I was going to keep her—or him, if that had been the case. Wait," she said. "I'll get you a photo."

Marsha got up, rocking the swing, and disappeared through the screen door.

"February 1965." Colton's head was spinning. "Twelve!"

Was her daughter his, and she'd never said anything to him, not a word?

No! Could it be?

The thought that perhaps Abby could be his daughter hit him so hard, he stood up, jerking the swing so violently it hit the back of his knees.

When was that night? But it had only been one night—graduation? They had been so happy, so much in love, and yes, they had gotten carried away that night. They'd gone farther than they had ever gone before. But could it have happened with only the one time?

Obviously, it could.

He was still standing, stunned by the realization that

Abby could be his when Marsha came back, carrying a photo in a frame and a photo album.

When Colton saw the photo of Abby, he no longer doubted. Abby looked just like he did at that age, only a girl. She also looked just like his mother did at that age. The female gene passed down. But would Marsha admit it to him? He only knew he had to find out.

"Marsha," he began, and something about the tone of his voice caused her to look up at him, to where he was staring at his daughter's photo.

Blue eyes met his unwaveringly.

She's waiting for me to discover it, he thought.

"She's mine, isn't she? Abby's mine. I have a daughter, have had a daughter for twelve years, and never knew it. Why didn't you tell me?"

The anguish and longing in his voice brought tears to her eyes, but they never left his face.

"Because you were such a noble, upright young man. You would have immediately wanted to 'do the right thing' by me, and insisted on marrying me. That would have put you working in some factory in Fort Smith to support your family. You would have hated it. And you would have quickly resented me as the cause of your frustrations and ended up hating me. Our marriage would not have survived. Besides, my grandmother always told me if I ever got pregnant to never marry the father, because it never worked out. Remember Andy and Sue, or even Rick and Jane, ahead of us in school? It didn't work for them. You needed college and the freedom to go there. I had a part of you with me. I knew I would always love you and your child."

"Oh, Marsha, how I love you," he had whispered, drawing her close. I know now that's why I never married, because I've always loved you. And now, I have a daughter to love."

❧❧❧

Present Day:

That was six years ago, but he still remembered every word as if it were yesterday. Now here was this same beautiful daughter, obviously in distress.

Never one to hesitate when he knew what his course of action must be, Colton turned and reached for the phone. He would have his men start a search for and find the red Camaro he saw them drive away in.

He instructed the patrol cars to stop the Camaro when they spotted it and call him, but only during their free time. This was not anything he could use department time on. And he wanted to personally be there.

He knew he was risking having a rebellious teenager on his hands, if even for the inane, simple reason that she would think it was embarrassing in front of a new boyfriend and possibly in front of other friends, but at this point, he didn't care.

He had heard her cry for help and help he would, whatever the cost to her ego.

He would find out why she was afraid of this young man and what she was hiding behind her smile.

He had opened his mouth to ask who or where, but she was gone so quickly, the screen door banging shut behind her. As he stood there unable to move, the car roared away.

Again, he wondered what it was she started to say.

Chapter 8

"Commander?"

"Yo!" Colton called out, turning away from the map on the wall.

"Call for you. Line three."

"Thanks."

"Colton Mitchell here."

"This is Lonnie."

"Lonnie? Oh, yeah, Lon, what's up? How's Nancy?"

"She's better, but still in the hospital."

It was only the day after Nancy had been admitted. Colton had not expected to hear from the kid so soon.

"I was able to talk to the two guys who were sitting across the street."

"And? Did they know the guy?"

"Well, that's strange. Very funny. They say they didn't see anyone. Said they saw Nancy come down the street, because they commented on how she looked, and how pretty she used to be." Here his voice cracked, and he paused. "It's always painful to see someone you love abusing themselves, letting themselves slip farther and farther into self-abuse." Lon took a deep breath. "Anyway, they said that when she got to the corner of the building she stopped and seemed to be talking to herself. She reached out her hand, seemed to take something from the air and put it in her mouth. They said they shook their heads, still talking about her and what drugs had done to her."

"Didn't anyone ever want to help her, down there?" Colton asked.

Did you? Lon wanted to ask Colton, as a policeman, but he knew better than to say anything like that. "Well…" he began. "She belonged to Sammie. And I say 'belonged' because I've already made arrangements to take her out of here. You said she needed someone to love her and take care of her. Well, I'm going to take her home with me just as soon as she gets dismissed. We've talked, and she knows. She wants to change. She's just been weak, you know."

"Where are you taking her? We might need her as a material witness. Right now, she's our only witness, only clue we have to all these killings."

"I called home," Lon admitted. "After all these years away, I called home. I said some pretty terrible things to my folks the day I walked away. I didn't think they would ever want me back again. But Mom and Dad both cried. They were so happy to hear from me, to know I'm okay. When I explained about Nancy, they said she was more than welcome to come, that they would love her, too."

Lon's voice had cracked about halfway through. Colton suspected the young man was crying, but he would never let on that he knew.

"And where is home?" Colton asked.

"Tucson. They never suspected I was so close. They said they figured I'd run away to L.A. or New York."

"I may need her," Colton said. "I'll only let you take her if I can get you at any time. I don't want her disappearing on me. Let me have your parents' phone number, and I'll call them."

"You mean you really could keep me from taking her home with me?"

"Lon, this thing is much more serious than you can ever imagine. It's not just a simple case of a young lady almost OD'ing. There's more involved. I just can't tell you, man, although I'd like to. But believe me when I tell you she's our only, and I do mean only, clue to a murderer."

There was silence on the other end of the line. Lon could find nothing to say in response. He hadn't realized or thought about how serious this was. His thoughts had only been on Nancy. "You've got it. The phone number, I mean," he finally answered.

"Now, back to the subject," Colton continued. "What you're telling me, Lon, is that these men probably recognized the pusher, but don't want to say anything. Is that it?"

"No, Commander. Really. I made sure they weren't just jiving me. They were speaking true, 'cause they thought it was strange, too, 'cause Nancy had never done anything like that before. They swear they didn't see anyone else there, no one at all, just Nancy talking away to herself. But my question is, if no one was there, then who did Nancy get the bad junk from? And, oh, by the way, did you know she had a couple more of them?"

"Oh, really?" Colton asked, sitting up in his chair, causing the front legs to hit the floor. "No, I didn't know. Where are they now?"

He should have thought of that. But since it was not a crime scene, just left as the paramedics found her in the apartment, the place would not have been searched for anything, not at the time, anyway.

He could almost see the young man on the other end

of the line frowning, thinking about the pills, then shrugging.

"I don't know," Lon said. "I guess they're probably still on the floor of her apartment. I saw them fall out of her hand when she grabbed her throat the first time. No one's been there, so I guess they'd be there somewhere on the floor."

"You said you had a key, didn't you?" Colton asked.

Here was probably the first real and certainly would be the most important clue they would have so far in these cases. If these pills could be analyzed, the manufacturer and areas of the country where the ingredients were from, that sort of thing could be pinpointed. They had all sorts of ways of tracing the origins of the ingredients.

"Where are you now?" Colton asked him.

"I'm back at the hospital. I want to be here when she wakes up."

The young lady was not out of the danger zone completely. A thought occurred to Colton. If this killer found out she was alive and thought she could probably identify him, he might try to get to her, shut her up before she recovered enough to talk to the police. As of yet, however, he probably didn't know she had pulled through. They were keeping this quiet, no press leaks so far.

"I need you to meet us at Nancy's. We need to find the other pills, analyze them. They could lead us to the killer."

There was silence on the other end. He didn't want to leave his girl.

Killer? Lon wondered. *Didn't Nancy just OD? What is going on?*

"Look, she's in good hands, the best of care. You can either come voluntarily, or I'll order you to."

That seemed to clinch the deal.

"Okay, I'm leaving right now. Give me a half hour to get there."

The young man hung up on him, showing his contempt. You couldn't be arrested for hanging up the phone, but it spoke volumes.

Colton would have to watch himself with this one. At best, he was a very reluctant witness and helper. Colton didn't need him to clam up completely. He had a feeling he was going to need him, still, on the street. Yet, the young man knew just how far to go with a cop without crossing that certain invisible line that would get him into trouble.

Chapter 9

Colton was not as familiar with the part of the city where Nancy lived as with other parts of Denver, so he took another officer with him, one from that area.

The speech, the mannerisms, the way of walking would be familiar to the other officer.

They had farther to go than Lon, so when they got to the address, Lon was standing outside an old brownstone apartment building, waiting for them.

Colton glanced around, spotting two men sitting across the street. Chances were, they were the same two who had seen Nancy score. He would talk to them later.

"It's pretty bad in there," Lon said, when they approached him.

They looked at him questioningly.

"Nancy threw up all over the place. When the ambulance arrived, I just closed and locked the door behind me. I haven't been back till now. I'll clean up when you leave."

"Roommate?"

He shook his head.

"No, Nancy lived here alone. I stayed when she let

me, but no one else ever did. Her johns were usually in and out pretty quick."

"We've seen some pretty rough stuff," Colton said.

Lon just shrugged. Tough-nut cops, of course. He turned and jogged down five or six steps to a basement apartment.

Although he had been warned, Colton still wasn't prepared for the stench that assaulted them when Lon opened the door. They recoiled, stepping back a step or two.

Lon grinned at them. He had warned them, after all. Maybe they weren't as tough as they thought they were.

Bad ass cops, huh? he thought. He pulled the door shut.

"Tell you what. I'll clean this mess up," he volunteered. "Want to wait?"

"Sure," Colton answered. He had an idea. "We'll just go across the street. Are those the two men who saw Nancy?"

"Yeah, but good luck," Lon retorted.

"What do you mean?"

"They're pretty hard asses when it comes to cops. Don't be surprised if they won't talk. They talked to me because I belong here, on this street, and they know how I feel about Nancy."

Colton nodded. He understood the attitude. If would be simply because they were cops. They may even know the guy who gave Nancy the stuff but would never put themselves in the position of telling. At least not openly so anyone could see.

Instead of going across the street immediately, Colton and James stood outside the apartment. They stood there quite a while, watching the activity on the street. They decided to talk to the two men on the steps.

The two men had watched them approach. They

were instantly wary. They could tell a cop from down the street.

His partner stopped them before they crossed the street. James had an idea that might get the men talking. They probably expected the two cops to walk right over to them, flashing badges, showing who they were, tossing around a little weight. So, they would do something different to get their attention.

Colton and James walked slowly across the street and down past the two men, simply nodding at them as they passed by.

The two men nodded back. Then they looked at each other as the two men walked by. They were already curious.

The two cops stopped opposite the playground, but still across the street from it. As usual, a small group of young teen-age boys were playing hoop. If these kids couldn't buy anything else, they somehow managed to always have a good basketball.

Some things were just important.

Colton held his head close to the other, and they talked in low tones, gesturing and pointing to the building across the street as they did so.

After several minutes, one of the men got up and started toward them. This was what James had hoped for. He was playing on the curiosity of the man as to what they were saying. He also relied on the fact that these men would want to show that they knew something the cops didn't. If they approached Colton and James first, then the cops were over their first hurdle, although the men would not realize they were falling in with the plan.

Colton sensed one of them had stopped a few feet away.

"Hey, you guys here about Nancy?" the man asked a few minutes later, not being able to stand being ignored.

James turned toward him, not answering right away. "Could be, man," he said. That was part of the plan, too. James was from here and could communicate. "What you know?"

The man shrugged, playing the game. "Nothing much. Hell, she just came shuffling up the walk yesterday, then stopped there at the corner of that building." At first, he pointed and drew his finger in a line as he showed how Nancy came down the sidewalk. Then he pointed at the building across the street. "She just stood there, talking to herself, reaching out, taking things out of the air. We wondered what she was on, some bad trip or something. We've seen her out of it before, but this was plain spooky. She put her hands to her mouth like she put something in her mouth. She put her head back like she was swallowing something. She was sure acting crazy, man. Really out of it, you know?"

"Yeah, I know. So, there was no one else there, huh?" James asked.

"You're the second one asked that. Lon did earlier. What's going on, anyway? We said there was no one, so what's with the questions? Don't you believe us? Do I look like I need glasses or something?"

The man was getting defensive, thinking people were going to think he was lying or something. He knew what he saw—or didn't see.

"Sure. No problem. See anything else unusual?"

The man shrugged. "Just a U-Haul. And that's sort of unusual, you know? Not too many people around here can afford to pay for a U-Haul. They just bring things— furniture and such—in a pickup or even make several trips with stuff in their trunks. It was a pretty new one, too. Didn't stay long, though, 'cause it might not have had its wheels for too long, you know." The man grinned. That was just what happened in this neighborhood.

"And where was it parked?" James asked, casually. He didn't want to show any undue interest in the vehicle, but he had seen Colton stiffen at the mention of it, so perhaps it was important.

James was on the team investigating those drug overdoses that were shaping up like serial killings, so he knew that any little detail might be important to the investigation. "You remember which building they were moving in or out of?" he asked.

The other man had walked up in time to hear this last question. The two men looked at each other.

The first man had turned to the other man. "Didn't see nobody moving in or out of nowhere. Did you?"

The second man shook his head.

"How long had you been sitting on the steps?" James asked.

This seemed amusing to the two men. They laughed.

"Been sittin' there most our lives, I guess," the second one said, grinning.

James nodded his head, showing he understood what they were saying.

"But yesterday? Maybe the people in the U-Haul saw something, if we could find out the apartment."

They both shrugged.

"U-Haul just pulled up and sat there. The driver must have got out the other side, gone in someplace we couldn't see for the U-Haul. Never saw anyone around the truck. Did we?" he asked the other man again.

"Yeah, I actually did, once," the other man said.

"You did? When was that? You ain't said nothing to me about it, man."

"So, the driver didn't get out the driver's side, which is the one you could see?"

"So, what did you see?" asked James.

"Funny thing. I just casually strolled by, you know.

Didn't want to really seem like I was looking at another man's stuff, you know."

James nodded. He understood. You really didn't get too involved or nosy in this part of town.

"All I saw was lots of boxes. He man was bent over one of the boxes. As he straightened up, I saw him holding two jars in his hands. You know, those clear kind with the screw on lids."

"Mason jars?" Colton asked. Somehow, he remembered those from his childhood.

The man shrugged.

"Whatever you want to call 'em. All I saw in them were sticks and weeds. At least it looked like that to me. I thought they were the strangest drugs, or maybe ingredients for weed or something, that I had ever seen. But if a man wants to make his own stuff, he can, that's what I thought. Maybe something new was going to start on the street."

"But you didn't see him get out with the jars or do anything with them?"

"No," the man said. "Yes. I mean, yes, that the side we could see, and no, no one ever got out that way. Maybe he got out the back, but I was passed by that time. Didn't want to seem too interested," he repeated.

"And where was it exactly?"

Both men pointed and gestured down the street.

"Then you didn't see who got out to it, who got in it later and drove away? And when did they drive away? Did you see that?"

The two men frowned, obviously thinking, trying to remember. They looked at each other. It seemed that each one expected the other to know the answer. After all, they were sitting on the steps the whole time, just yards up the street. All they did every day, all day long, was sit and watch what went on along that street.

That was their life.

They could tell you when each girl had each trick, how long certain ones took, who stopped and shopped where and when. They knew everyone and everything that went on.

But they had not seen this pusher, or what they thought was a new pusher with his own stuff, and now there were trying to remember having seen the driver of the U-Haul.

One finally answered.

"I think it pulled away just as Lon was running up from the apartment, upstairs. Lon was yelling for someone to call an ambulance. Fred, here, and I jest stood up, watching Lon, wondering out loud to each other as to what was going on. Must have been then the U-Haul pulled away."

"Yeah," the other man agreed, "'cause a few minutes later the ambulance got here, pulled in at the same spot. U-Haul had to be gone. Ain't that right, Jackson?"

Each man looked to the other for affirmation. But it was obvious that neither man remembered exactly when it left or who had been driving it.

"Ain't you guys got ways of checking those things?" Jackson asked Colton, who was standing closest to him.

Check U-Hauls? What did these guys think the police were? Supermen? There was no way to check on every U-Haul in the Denver area. And considering the fact that a person usually had five days rental on the trucks for moving time, the thing could be from anywhere in the country and back there by now, too.

"Too many U-Hauls."

"Did you see the license plate number?"

"Didn't even think to look," the first man said. "Can you check those?"

"Too many," Colton answered, simply, in a neutral

tone. No use telling the man what a dumb idea it was.

"Last thing we saw was Nancy and Lon getting into the ambulance. Thought she was probably a goner, for sure. She okay?"

"Yeah, she's gonna be fine," James responded.

The men nodded, satisfied. They saw nothing unusual in the questions the men had been asking them.

"You guys reckon it was some of that weed stuff that new man was pushing?"

These guys might be smarter than they looked, thought James.

"Don't know. Just asking about everything on the street around that time, you know?" answered James.

"Yeah, just your job, huh?"

"You got it. Let us know if you think of anything else, okay?"

The group broke up, with Colton and James walking back across the street to Nancy's apartment.

They would have to think about what they had just heard later. Maybe something would be important. Who knew?

❦❦❦

Lon was just coming back out of the apartment. He motioned to them to enter. He had scrubbed the floors and bathroom where Nancy had been ill. Even with the windows open, there was still an underlying stench beneath the pine smell. This would take several more cleanings.

Lon held out his hand to Colton, opening it to reveal three capsules. Colton took them with his handkerchief, handling them very carefully. By now they probably would not have any discernible fingerprints on them, but he used required procedures, anyway.

The capsules were orange and white, generic. No company or brand name appeared on the outside. They still contained an orange powder, though, and that was what they were after. That was what Jack, the chief medical examiner, needed to determine what was killing these people. That was traceable.

"Let's get these to Jack right now. I want to know what's in this. I want to know what's in it that kills," Colton concluded. He turned to Lon. "You'll let us know if you find out anything else, if anyone else says anything or hears anything on the street about yesterday?"

Lon nodded his head. "Are you going past the hospital?" he asked, hopefully. "Can you drop me off? I hitched a ride here, but I want to go back and be with Nancy again."

"Sure, why not?" Colton said. It wouldn't hurt them to help. This young man would remain a cooperative witness if they showed they were willing to help.

They all left in the unmarked squad car, which would no longer be unmarked in this area.

Colton felt they were being watched by many pairs of eyes as they pulled away from the curb, even beyond those of the two men they had talked to.

Was one pair of eyes the one they needed to locate? He didn't have any feelings about it, so he figured the man was clear across the city by now. The man was probably planning his next attack.

Chapter 10

Jack shook his head. "I don't know. I really honestly don't know. I'm at a loss. There is nothing in my forensic parameters I can compare it to. I've even done the computer analysis trying to find a match of any known substances." As chief medical officer, Jack had used all the equipment in the pathology lab to run every test he could think of on the contents of the capsule Colton had brought to him earlier in the day.

"Substance?" Colton questioned. "What are we talking about here?"

"Drugs," Jack answered. "A drug. The only definite common denominator is the cause of death. All these victims have died from a drug overdose. I have no explanation, though. I don't know its name. I don't know where it's coming from. Obviously, it's coming off the streets, and that's a problem for you guys. But, again, I don't know what it is, so I can't tell you the manufacturer or any of the ingredients.

"Let me show you, Colton."

Jack tapped in a few keys on the computer and the chemical composition of the substance appeared on the monitor.

"Now, you can pull up every other composition of every known drug, and you will not match this. You can definitely take my word on that."

Jack waved his hand toward the monitor.

"So, what are you telling me?" Colton asked. "Are we talking aliens or something?"

Jack laughed at Colton, but he continued to look him straight in the eye.

"I don't have a clue," Jack said. "All I know is that this substance is definitely killing these people. Can we expect more? What's your gut feeling? Do you guys have any leads yet? Are you any closer to finding the murderer?"

"No, in fact—" Colton began then stopped. "What do you mean 'murderer'? We suspected a killer, maybe several killers, but aren't these just bad drugs?"

Jack shrugged. "It's someone, or several someones, using the same drug."

Colton decided to confide in his friend. "If it's murder, there's one he hasn't killed."

"Oh, yeah?" Jack asked expectantly.

"The young lady who took these—" Colton nodded toward the slide. "—was rushed to the hospital yesterday. Turned out she'd OD'd. Her boyfriend had called it in. Lucky he was there with her or she wouldn't have made it. He forced her to drink some spoiled milk, and she upchucked everything. But her lips had started to take on an orange tint. There was even an orange glow under her fingernails. Whatever it is, it sure acts quickly."

"But she didn't die?"

"No, in fact, she's still in the hospital. She pulled through, but she's very weak. I haven't had an opportunity to talk with her yet about who she got the stuff from. The boyfriend thought he saw the man, but he's not sure."

"What do you mean he's not sure?" Jack asked. "You either see an exchange, or you don't. Right?"

"Well, I'm not so sure about that," Colton admitted. "The guy remembers seeing the girl reach out and take something from someone, but the other person must have been in the shadows of a building or something."

"I need to talk to this girl."

"I haven't had time to talk to you about it," Colton responded. "I had just been home for a few minutes this morning to shower and change clothes and had some 'words,' shall we say, with Abby. She stomped out of the house with her new boyfriend. Then the telephone rang."

"You? Sharp words with Abby?" Jack asked, incredulously. "I thought you two were the perfect father/daughter combination."

"Well, she's been acting a little strange lately, and I'm really not sure what's wrong with her. If I weren't completely confident that Abby knows right from wrong, I'd say she's acting like someone on drugs. And, you know, she's lost a lot of weight.

"I had a phone call just as she left. It was the vice-principal at her school. She hasn't been showing up for classes, turning in homework, or showing up for cheerleading practice. She's just not interested in any of her clubs. She hasn't even been doing the DARE Program."

"What?" Jack said, surprised. "No DARE? That was Abby's *pet* project. Something *has* to be going on with her."

Colton had not been quite ready for someone else to tell him something was wrong with Abby. He hadn't quite formulated his own thoughts about the situation himself.

"Well, I don't know. Teenagers have these phases. They go through stages. There's a need to show their independence with little rebellions here and there. After all, she's eighteen. We just have to live through them."

"What about this weight loss?" Jack asked. "Tell me about that."

Jack might be the medical examiner, a pathologist and forensic expert doing all the autopsies, but he was still first and foremost a family physician.

"Well, in the last…month, at least…she hasn't been around for dinner. She always had other commitments. She used to always have dinner with Marsha and me. You know that. As you said, we had a great family time together. We'd talk about our day and what was happening. She'd enjoy hearing about my cases, at least as much as I felt I could talk about them. We always had a good time around the table. As I said, she hasn't been showing up for dinner. She's losing weight rapidly. In fact, I've brought you something that she seems to be living on instead of regular food. I have to admit I haven't been a very dutiful father lately what with these particular overdoses going on. And now you're trying to tell me they're murders. Let me show you something she carries in her purse and really enjoys."

Colton felt around in his inside jacket and brought out the orange-striped candy stick.

"*Orange*?" asked Jack. He sounded excited.

"Yes, this is what she eats all the time."

"Would you let me examine that?"

"That's exactly why I brought it," Colton said. "I don't know why, but the color orange stuck in my mind. What about the orange glow under the fingernails and the orange tint to the lips? And now orange candy."

"It will only take me a few minutes. Why don't you stick around and let's see what we can find out," Jack said.

"Sure."

He stood still and calm while Jack put the powdered

candy through some tests. After a few minutes, he walked around the spotless room. Considering the type of work that was done here, the place was immaculate. It smelled of disinfectant.

Now, I bet that's a big inventory item, Colton thought as he spotted a bottle of disinfectant. He didn't touch anything.

Jack had his personal notebook open on a counter. Colton paused and looked down at it. It obviously contained some notes that only Jack understood.

Letters, mostly.

Colton shook his head. That seemed just like Jack.

A few minutes later, Jack motioned to him.

"Come here, take a look at this."

Colton could tell by the tone of his voice that Jack was agitated and excited about something.

Colton walked around to the computer.

"Oh, you matched it with something. That's good. What is it? Kool-Aid candy?"

"No, I wish it were as simple as that. We wouldn't have a problem here."

Jack was looking at Colton, very concerned.

The same feeling Colton had before, hit him in the pit of the stomach.

"Well?" Colton asked. "What did you find?"

"This…" Jack said, waving his hand at the computer monitor. He couldn't seem to find the right words. "…this is the same unknown drug that's been in these bodies. It's what killed these seven people."

The silence was deafening. The only sound was the hum of the computer. Colton was stunned. He couldn't believe what he was hearing. He had the sudden feeling he was falling down the rabbit hole like Alice.

"You're kidding," Colton said, incredulously. "How could that be? It's candy."

Colton zoned. His brain seemed to have gone numb.

"Colton, Colton. Are you listening to me?"

Colton realized Jack was still speaking. But he had been lost deep in his own thoughts. He shook his head and returned his attention to Jack. "Well, it's packaged like candy. It smells like candy, and it may even be marketed and palmed off as candy, but it's definitely the drug in question. Some pusher is handing this stuff out. I hate to say this to you, but we've been friends a long time. The situation you've described sounds like Abby may be hooked. Her continual need for this candy, her weight loss, and her general attitude are symptomatic of a serious addiction. Colton, you need to deal with this right away. Find out where it's coming from. What about her friends?"

Jack was continuing, not giving Colton a chance to respond, which was just as well. He was speechless. He was speechless with the facts that Jack found, but also that he was right about his suspicions about Abby.

"You're going to let me keep the rest of this, aren't you? I need to run some corroborating tests. But I would swear on it as an expert witness. I'd even stake my reputation on it. This is what's killing people. If it's coming from the same pusher, is he, or she, aware of what's happening? Would it be possible to get more?"

"I don't know," Colton responded. "This just happened to fall out of Abby's purse while we were having our…heated discussion, shall I say…right before she rushed out. She'd laid her purse down and several items, including these candy sticks, fell out. She grabbed them up, jamming the sticks back in her purse. One didn't get all the way in and slipped out again. She didn't notice it fall to the floor. She'd made a point a few minutes before that, though, of making sure the candy sticks were out of sight and back into her purse. That's why I—I picked it up and kept it after she left. It all seemed so important to her. She had been so possessive of them. And for some reason, the color *orange* just keeps popping into my mind. There are so many unanswered questions about it."

"I can answer one question," Jack said. "This is the killer drug." He held up several small vials containing the tainted tissue from the bodies. "It's here, in these samples. Here, take one of these vials. Souvenir," he grinned wickedly.

Colton reached out and took it, absented mindedly putting in a pocket of his jacket.

Then Jack became serious. "And, Colton?"

"Yeah?" Colton knew what Jack was about to say. *So, say it.*

"You know you need to get it away from Abby, don't you? The sooner, the better. Which brings up an interesting question."

"What's that?" Colton asked.

"If this drug is killing others, and so quickly, then why hasn't it killed Abby? Is she just not getting as much as the others, at least not all at one time? And if she's not getting as much as the others, then why not? Why shouldn't she be?"

Jack looked steadily at Colton, a frown between his eyes. He was asking the questions of himself as much as he was of Colton.

Colton was at a loss for words. Jack had thought the same thing about a split second before he did. They almost thought of it at the same time.

Why wasn't Abby getting enough of the drug to overdose? She was only getting enough at one time to make her lose weight, lose interest in her activities, lose interest in her life as she knew it, and be rebellious with her father.

Good question. Why?

Jack told him he was the only one who knew of these findings, because Jack wanted to double-check everything before making a report. Colton left Jack's lab with the question unanswered. He was determined to confront Abby that evening when she came back from her date with this new boyfriend of hers.

They agreed to meet at the hospital in an hour. Jack had a few loose ends he wanted to tie up before he was gone from the lab for a while.

Chapter 11

Colton saw Jack get out of his car in the physician's area of the hospital parking lot. "Jack, wait up!" Jack turned when he heard his friend's voice. He glanced down at his watch as Colton approached.

"Kind of early, even for you," he commented.

"Not lately," Colton responded. "Not since this serial killer started his thing with that unknown drug of yours."

"His?" Jack asked. "Are you sure?"

They walked toward the hospital entrance.

⁓⁓⁓

The man leaned against a tree in the small park that was part of the hospital grounds, adjoining the physicians parking lot. He desired to blend into, to become one with the tree trunk. To any passerby, he would not have attracted attention. For those who might see him, he casually held an open newspaper. He appeared to be waiting for someone.

He had waited overnight for Colton to leave his home so he could follow him. He saw another man join him in the hospital parking lot. He decided to touch him, see who he was, see what he meant to Colton. See if this man would serve his purposes, or if he needed to look further.

∽∾∽

Colton and Jack continued to walk toward the entrance of the hospital.

"No, actually, I'm not sure of anything in this case, or these cases, if you want to say that. I've never gone up against orange-tinted lips and fingernails before. For God's sake, what is it?"

He looked over at the man at his side.

Jack looked as if he hadn't slept in a week and then in the same clothes he had on now.

"Oh—" Jack exclaimed, stopping suddenly, reaching up to grab his head, starting to rub his temples. He staggered sideways slightly, toward Colton, and Colton instinctively reached out to steady him.

"What?" he asked. "Migraine hit you all at once?"

"I'd say yes, if I knew what a migraine headache felt like. I *never* have headaches."

He groaned again, holding his head still.

They had stopped halfway to the hospital from their cars.

"If this is a migraine, then I'll never, never judge another person's pain when they say they're suffering from one. Even Brad."

Brad was one of Jack's assistants, one who always had bad headaches.

"Come on into the hospital. We'll find a doctor and get something for that. Of course, they might want to give you an MRI just to prescribe aspirin, but we'll see."

"Whew," Jack said. "It seems to be passing now. Skip the doctor. I want to talk to that young lady."

They walked slowly into the hospital.

"Now, what were we talking about?"

"Something about the orange tint under the victims' fingernails…" Colton prompted.

"That's what I hope to find out from this girl. I would like to take a scraping of her fingernails. Even if they've washed her well, maybe some trace will show up. And I just hope she remembers something. Anything. You know, there's a possibility she was so doped up, she won't remember anything. Either that, or her brain is so already fried on drugs it won't let her remember."

"Yeah, I know."

The early morning bustle of a typical hospital had not subsided as they approached the room where Nancy was.

They were a few feet away when the door opened, and a nurse emerged.

She stopped when she saw them. "Sorry, officers, but we can't let you in there just now," she said, pleasantly.

Colton got the impression that her voice could change from soft to medium to hard very quickly if any given situation called for it.

"We only need to ask her a few questions," Jack countered.

"I've heard that one before," the nurse replied. "Anyway, she's getting a bath and a bed change, so it will have to be later." The tone of her voice told them she was going to have the final say.

"Oh," they both said at the same time.

"Coffee?" Colton asked.

"Sure," Jack agreed, "let's go down to the cafeteria. That vending machine crap literally makes me sick."

Colton laughed. "I know what you mean."

"Let's give 'em a good half hour. Surely then they can't have any more excuses."

"Oh, yeah? That's what you think, but tell me all you can about this girl."

They had gone through the line and were sitting outside the cafeteria area. A patio-type arrangement had been constructed for those who wanted to have their meals outside.

"Well, there's not that much, really. Only that she came in yesterday. Since the hospital has to let us know of a drug overdose, I got stuck with coming down to check it out. At least I felt it was just routine until I talked to the young man who came in with her. When I found out the condition and that she thought it was bad drugs and that the young man, Lon, knew there were more of the capsules, then I gave it more attention. That's where you came in, checking out the capsules and later Abby's candy."

"Having you find out all the deaths were from the same substance was a shock, let me tell you."

"But still not enough evidence to take to the chief," Jack said.

"Yes, it seems to take a lot for him," Colton agreed.

"There's a funny twist to these cases," said Jack.

"What do you mean?" Colton asked. He knew he was tired, but he thought he had thought of almost everything. It seemed to be the only thing he *did* think about these days, that and Abby, and now she seemed to be a part of it, too. Just where she fit in, he wasn't sure yet. And he didn't get to meet the new boyfriend this morning.

As he was shaving, the phone had rung. Marsha told him a few minutes later that Craig had called for Abby to meet him at school today, some family member borrowed the car or something like that.

Does he know I want to meet him? Colton had thought then dismissed it as crazy. How could the boy know?

A girlfriend had picked up Abby. She had gone in early, too, because Colton made it down to the kitchen.

Was she trying to avoid him? Did she not want to talk about the orange candy again?

Colton reached up, pushing his hair back from his face with his right hand. What were his thoughts doing this morning? They seemed to be leaping back and forth and around from one thought to another.

Boy, was he tired.

Jack glanced up at him. "I hate to tell you this, but we've been friends for a long time. You look like hell, old boy. Did you get any sleep last night? I would've thought you would have after we made such an important discovery."

"I haven't told anyone else, by the way. Just you. I wanted to see this girl, talk to her, before writing a report. But it's all in here," Jack said, as he held up his notebook for Colton to see.

"Yeah, good idea. And thanks for making me feel so good about my usually wonderful good looks. Are you telling me I wouldn't be much of a lady killer today?"

"Are you ever, you ugly thing?"

They both laughed, which was good for them. They needed to find some humor in this situation. A situation that was serious and seemed to be getting more so all the time.

This young lady in here was a definite warm lead to the killer. She was just that lucky to be alive. She was the only one so far.

That brought up some interesting questions, at least to Jack's mind.

"So, why not more?"

"Excuse me?" Colton asked.

"Overdoses. Why not more overdoses?"

Colton just looked at him, waiting, knowing Jack had something on his mind and he was about to hear it.

"If this drug is being sold on the street, then why not more, even deathly sick druggies, like Nancy here? Why just her? What do these have in common? Certainly not the part of town they are from. Come on, Colton. We've been friends a long time. Just because I'm a doctor now and not a detective upstairs, doesn't mean I can't know about this, about what's coming down here. What gives with this?"

Colton raised his coffee cup, looking at Jack over the top of it. He took a sip of the black juice. It was weak, but he didn't care. Maybe the hospital was trying to cut costs and stretch their coffee as far as it would go.

"No, that doesn't seem to be the connection, at least not in the way you're thinking," Colton agreed.

"Then, what?"

"They—the bodies—have been found in different parts of town," Colton began.

But his thoughts were a million miles away. There had been a series of deaths of homeless people around Denver. So far, no one in the police department did not know if all the slayings were connected or whether a copy cat was at work with some of them.

Most Denver residents wanted to believe the slayings happened in LoDo, a small section of downtown, because many people thought of that entire area as lower downtown.

There was pressure on the police department to solve the murders, especially from owners of the office buildings in LoDo. They had worked very hard to keep LoDo safe.

Coffee shops, breweries, cafes and even renovated

apartment buildings rented or sold as "lofts" all thrived near where one of the victims had been found.

Some owners were even friends of the homeless, offering them hot coffee and food. They thought the killings should have more people troubled and were angry at the apparent complacency about the crimes.

Some thought the police and downtown residents were trying to sweep the slayings under the rug. One owner voiced his opinion that he thought the police were not doing enough because the victims were not senators or public officials.

That wasn't the case. They just simply had no clues so far.

He brought his thoughts back to the present.

"You don't even know the half of it, yet," Colton said, taking another sip of the horrible coffee.

"I don't know any of it yet," Jack corrected. "That's what I'm hoping you'll do right now, let me in on the investigation so far."

Colton began, "I just didn't think that you would believe, either, or at least you won't believe what I think it is. It may not be that at all, but it's looking like. It really stretches the world of reality. But don't they say the truth is stranger than fiction? I believe it, because of something that happened before, but I really don't expect anyone else to believe it. Well, except Marsha and my brother Dan, of course. And I'll have to convince Abby. And that'll be hardest of all."

"And why haven't I heard of your brother, Dan, before?"

"Dan's my brother in Arkansas. We worked together to solve a case there six years ago."

"Before you moved here."

"Yeah. And it's not one of those things you talk about later, if only out of superstition."

"That bad, huh?"

"Different, at least," Colton agreed.

"So, you gonna tell me?"

Colton told Jack about the events of six years back.

Jack whistled softly.

"So, you're the target for revenge, or what, here?"

"Yes, I'm beginning to think so."

"You mean it's not the normal psycho wigged out because you arrested his uncle's cousin's brother for nearly killing someone and now he's trying to get back at you?"

Colton laughed. "Someone at the precinct asked something like that, also. But it's worse than that."

"How so?"

"It is revenge, that much is true. The killer was— is—trying to get my attention. And, believe me, he's got it."

"Oh, come on, Colton," Jack said. "We really don't have much time here, and I can't stand for you to leave me hanging like this."

A waiter came, and they both took a fresh cup of coffee, giving Colton a few seconds to try to organize his thoughts and decide how to begin to tell such an incredible story.

"Six years ago, Abby was kidnapped, and I was able to stop her from being killed, as seven other girls and boys had been over a twenty-year period of time, by the same killer. Dan and I were able to kill him. I guess I should correct that to say Dan was able to kill him as a thing…a man…whatever…attacked me. It's only a theory of mine and maybe not even a valid theory at all but I think it has something to do with that case. Now, he's coming after me, through somebody, maybe Abby, too, that's the other side to this orange drug business."

Colton stopped. That was it in a nutshell.

"That's it? That's all? Just how did he manage to get away? Didn't you say this brother of yours…Dan…killed him?"

As Jack was speaking, Colton had gone back six years in time. He heard Jack's voice, but not what he was saying.

He had lowered his head, resting it in his hands. He saw clearly the basement of the old house, Abby against the wall, unconscious. He saw clearly the pile of bones and felt he could taste the stench of the place.

He remembered Dan yelling at him. "Grab her, grab her, and run!"

It was as clear as if it were only yesterday.

He saw himself gather Abby into his arms and race back up the old stairs of the boarded-up house—

"Colton! Colton! Are you okay?" Jack had reached out to put a hand on Colton's arm, gently shaking him. "Hey, buddy, come back."

Colton raised his head, looking at his friend in surprise. He looked around the hospital grounds as if he didn't know where he was.

"Hey, you left us there for a few seconds, old boy. Where were you, anyway?"

"In another world, another time," Colton responded, smiling ruefully. "Sorry."

"No problem. You okay? I know you're tired. You need to go home, take it easy the rest of the day. I can talk to Nancy."

"Oh, no, I'm okay." Colton insisted. He looked down at his watch.

"In fact, we'd better go up. They should be finished in the room, and if we don't watch it, they'll be doing something else with her."

"I believe that," Jack agreed. He didn't like hospitals any more than Colton did. He realized the staff only tried to do their job, but he had never had an easy time trying to question patients when he needed to.

"I want to hear more about this deal of six years ago. You can't get away with just that much, you know."

"Sure, but later, okay? Let's get this over with and see if we can plan some way to stop this guy."

Jack was glad he was a few steps behind Colton so that Colton couldn't see the look on his face. Colton was serious about this being someone from his past seeking revenge.

Chapter 12

Nancy looked like a pale, ghostly skeleton as she lay still in the hospital bed. She was so thin, so gaunt that she seemed to have skin stretched over bone.

But her eyes, large blue eyes with dark, long lashes, were bright and the only indication that life still stirred in this wasted body.

Drugs had certainly taken their toll on her young body. Surely, they had scarred her soul as well.

She turned her head toward Colton and Jack as they entered the hospital room. Her eyes never left Colton's face as they approached her bed. Any other movement seemed to require too much energy. Her bony hands rested on top of her stomach, on top of the sheet.

Colton hoped that she would look upon her narrow escape from death as a second chance at life and enter a rehab program. Why didn't these young people take advantage of these programs, especially when the "state"—translated taxpayers—paid for them? He felt with proper care and food, she could fully recover from her ordeal.

They stopped at the side of her bed, looking down at her. They saw no hostility in her stare but even smiling seemed to be beyond the scope of her physical limitations. She seemed to need all her strength for breathing.

"Do you feel like answering a few questions?" Colton asked.

She nodded.

"This is Jack," he said, nodding toward Jack. "He is the county medical examiner, and in this case, the pathologist."

Colton felt the need to add that. He knew in some states and some counties the coroner really did not have to have any medical degree at all. In fact, they needed no medical knowledge at all. All they had to do was pronounce a person dead. He wanted her to know that Jack would know what he was talking about and looking for.

"Nancy, when you bought and then took the orange drug the other day, was that the first time you had taken that particular drug?"

"Yes," she whispered, shuddering.

Her voice was barely audible.

"Had you bought other drugs from this pusher before?"

"No," she again whispered in the same breathy voice.

"Was this the first time you had seen this man? It was a man, wasn't it?"

"Yes, to both," she said.

"Do you have a habit of buying from strange pushers?" Jack asked. He was going to lead up to some more important questions he wanted to ask.

"No, not at all. That's what's so..." She paused.

"What's so what?" Colton asked.

"Well, so...strange, I guess you'd say," she began.

They waited patiently. Nobody was going anywhere, and she needed to gather her breath between each sentence.

"I felt...drawn...to him somehow. And he seemed like a gentleman, especially when he called me a 'fair lady.' Nobody calls me anything nice anymore."

This long sentence led to a coughing spell, which caused the nurse to enter. She shook her head at them. "Enough for today," she said.

"But I haven't even started," Jack protested.

The nurse was already guiding them out. "Not today," she insisted.

Jack gave in to the inevitable.

☙❧

A few cars down, the man had been still for quite a while. He sat for a long time in the parking lot after Colton and Jack left.

He was growing weaker. He didn't know why, but it took more and more of an effort to keep up with Colton and Abby.

He couldn't make up his mind whether to kill them at the same time or separately. He couldn't decide who to destroy first, Abby or Colton.

He suddenly decided on Colton.

It had taken him a long time, years, in fact, to find Colton.

Finding Abby at the same time had been a bonus.

Now here was Colton, talking to another man, a man that seemed to have discovered his plan. That wouldn't do. It wouldn't do for Colton to find out too soon. He wanted to torture Colton, tease him, tantalize him, get to him through Abby, before...

The man couldn't understand what had gone wrong. He had been so careful, had used all his knowledge to come up with a foolproof plan to outwit the police.

Of course, he didn't want to completely outwit Colton. He wanted to play with him for a while. He wanted Colton to be smart enough to realize what was happening.

But what to do about the other man…Jack? This was a wild card that had been thrown into the deck.

How to play it?

He knew who Jack was because of the emblem on the side of the station wagon he had gotten into.

He knew where to find him.

Soon—soon.

Chapter 13

Colton drove home that evening with his thoughts on Abby. Although she had tried to appear the same, his daughter's actions were different from before.

From before what? a voice from somewhere asked him.

Exactly, he thought. *Before what?*

In his work, he was trained to watch a person's reactions to certain questions. Their responses usually gave them away, especially the guilty ones.

The truth he had to face was that Abby had acted guilty about something. He had seen it in her face, her actions. It was in the way she wouldn't quite meet his eyes when talking to him. What that something could be, he did not know. But that's what he was going to find out.

Sergeant Adamson was the policeman assigned this semester to go to the schools with the DARE program. The meetings were usually set up through Abby and the other officers at school. Colton would talk to Adamson on Monday, see now the program was going.

Abby certainly had the characteristics of someone on drugs. But could it really be?

How could he not have seen the signs of drug, and maybe even physical, abuse in Abby?

How many classes and training sessions had he attended through the department, to be able to spot this kind of behavior in suspects? Hell, how many training sessions had he lead at the many middle and high schools around the Denver area, urging any teenager, whether girl or boy, to speak up about abuse and seek help.

He had just been too close to Abby to see.

She had tried to act natural, but he felt the emotional detachment this morning. He had sensed the irritability in her at just talking to him. It was like he was keeping her from something important, something more important than talking to him, which certainly did not seem to be taking place lately.

What had happened to all their comfortable conversations, about any subject she could bring up?

Colton decided he would talk to this Craig, explain the situation. If Abby had the good judgment she always had, he would be an intelligent young man. He would understand that Abby needed more time to catch up on her schoolwork and he would not call or come by so often. Colton wanted to convince himself that this was the case.

After leaving a note to Marsha, Colton also began cruising, watching for the Camaro.

The conversation with Paul Mitchell only reinforced Colton's recognition of all the symptoms he was seeing of drug abuse and...perhaps...physical abuse? She was now doing so poorly in school when she had always been a straight A—almost—student.

His Abby, who always had been so outspoken against drugs, could she really have gotten involved somehow? Yet she knew the ploys of the pushers so well, had been trained by him and others what to look out for. She knew how to go beyond the "just say no" slogan that had been so popular several years back.

Could she be saved in time? Was it not too late for an intervention, whatever kind that might need to be? Perhaps there would be no long-lasting effects from this incident, which he felt could be attributed to this new boyfriend of hers. He had no real reason for sending the whole force looking for the red sports car, but he could call a few special friends, those in his squad who were not on duty right now. And he knew they would do it for him, without question.

He put his idea into motion. Within minutes he had called several men and knew they would do as he asked. In their own cars, they would start cruising this area looking for the red Camaro. When they spotted it, they would pull it over and call him. Surely, they would find her.

As Colton drove around, he decided to call Sarah, Abby's good friend. They had been best friends these last six years since they had lived in Denver. So, if anything was going on with Abby, he felt sure Sarah would know what it was and why.

He pulled over at a telephone booth, remembering the number from past times at the car pool for school.

Sarah answered on the second ring.

"Hi, Sarah. It's Mr. Mitchell. You know, Abby's dad."

"Oh, hi, Mr. Mitchell. How're you? How're things going?"

"Oh, just fine." He wanted to scream, *not very good, I'm falling apart with worry about Abby.*

But he didn't.

Sarah thought nothing about Colton calling. Both sets of parents were good friends. They had barbecues together, played cards together, so she thought nothing about this.

"Do you need to talk to Mom or Dad?" she asked.

"No, actually, I wanted to talk to you, Sarah."

He felt the pause in her mind. The loyalty of these kids to each other was amazing. They would never do or any anything to rat on each other or tell on each other, especially to parents or teachers. He knew he was going to have to tread softly and phrase his words and questions in a certain way, or he would never get any info from her.

"I'm calling about Abby, actually, and I thought maybe you might be able to help me with something."

"Well, sure, maybe, I guess so," Sarah said.

Again, he felt the hesitation more than heard it.

"She's lost some weight, you know, and her mom and I have been talking about that, and, doesn't she have lunch with you? She used to, always."

"Well, she did, with me, or with the group and everybody, but not since—" Sarah paused.

"Not since what?"

"Now that she's been going with Craig, she's been spending all her time with him. She really hasn't been doing much with us for a month or so now, maybe longer."

"Do you know where she's been having lunch and hanging out?"

He always admired the fact that the school had an "open lunch" policy, allowing the students to go eat wherever they wanted to, but now he wished it didn't.

"I really don't know."

"She really seems to enjoy this orange candy that she carries around with her all the time. What about that?"

"Oh, that's just orange Kool-Aid candy pixy sticks that we all have." Sarah sounded relieved. Here was something simple she could talk about. "Actually, it was

Abby who got everyone started. It's been a lot of fun, and became a fad with different groups. Different groups at school eat different colors. Abby got us started on orange, of all things, because I know she doesn't even like the color orange, and so, that's all we need. Other groups around school have red ones, green ones, you know. It's just one of those silly things that seem to go around, but it's going on, anyway."

"Where do you buy this candy, Sarah?"

"Oh, we mostly get it from the convenience store around the corner from the school, Johnson's. You know which one I mean, that little store on Fourth and Main. The little old couple that is always in there? We've probably increased their income a lot just buying this candy. In fact, he asked about it and made sure he ordered an extra supply just for the kids from Middleton. Different colors and flavors, of course." She giggled.

"Yeah, I know the store you mean, the little mom-and-pop store. Is that the only place you buy it?"

"Well, sometimes if we're at the mall, we'll pick it up at Mr. Bulky's, and that lasts awhile."

That answered one question, at least. Maybe Mr. Johnson wasn't a pusher in disguise.

"What about Abby? Does she always buy it with you guys? Do you know?"

"Well, actually, now that you mention it, Abby has never been with us. I think…" She paused, and Colton could almost picture the look on her face as she thought about Abby. "…I think…it seems like Craig always has some, and he gives it to her," she continued. "She always has some, there's no problem there. She doesn't buy it with us, though. Did I mention she doesn't even have lunch with us, not anymore?"

"Yes," Colton said.

"I thought she was into this getting skinny business,

you know, but I told her was getting a little too skinny. Her cheerleader outfit just hangs on her now. I guess she must be eating lunch off campus with Craig."

Colton wanted to pursue one subject at a time, find out as much as he could about her habits.

"Oh, she's been making cheerleader practice? How's that going, anyway, with you guys?"

"Well…actually, she hasn't been making cheerleader practice, not every time, anyway. And she seems so indifferent now, as if she doesn't care at all, and cheering was such a passion for her. She loves—loved—loves it."

Sarah sounded almost choked up about her friend.

There was another hesitation again. Colton knew that her friend did not want to tell things on her, for any reason at all. These kids were careful not to get their friends in trouble. That just would not do at all, especially if it got back to Abby that Sarah was the one who "snitched."

"Don't worry, Sarah, I'm not going to tell Abby that you've told me any of these things, but it is very important, anything you can tell me about Abby. We'll see that Abby gets fattened back up a little bit, okay? Next time you're with her, buy her a cheeseburger and French fries or something like that for us, okay? Then her mother and I won't worry so much."

Sarah laughed, as he had wanted her to. "That's a deal, and I'll even pay for it, too, Mr. Mitchell."

"You do that. And thanks for all your help, Sarah. Have a good time in school, you hear."

"Sure. Bye, Mr. Mitchell."

The conversation with Sarah worried him.

Chapter 14

Why was Colorado Boulevard so crowded this evening? One of his men had spotted a red Camaro with two young people sitting in it. Why didn't these cars get out of his way? It seemed that every car was deliberately going slow or stopping in front of him.

His instructions to watch and wait were obeyed. He wanted to be the one to confront his daughter.

It was there. The red car was still in place.

It was Abby, but they did not seem like a carefree, happy couple. In fact, they looked too serious. Where loud music should have been blaring from the car's speakers, there was silence. When they should have been laughing, they were silent. Abby was staring into the young man's eyes. Was he hypnotizing her? Had he brainwashed her, like some weird cult thing? Was he making her do these things?

Stop it, he chided himself. There was his imagination again.

Colton had to smile at himself, though. His mother would have called that "moon eyes" when a young lady looked that way.

Yet something was wrong with this picture. The bad feeling, which had died down earlier, now came back with a vengeance. It was a feeling like nothing he had ever had before.

He took that back. He did have this feeling once before. Six years before. It was the same feeling he'd had when he knew his daughter was missing, kidnapped by someone who murdered the girls and boys he kidnapped. Yes, it was the same feeling. To have the same feeling six years apart was really weird.

He parked his car on an adjacent street, walking toward the Camaro from the back, signaling to his friend to join him on the way.

Whatever the two young people were discussing, they were so deep in thought that Colton and Pete were able to come alongside the car on each side before the passengers realized it.

Craig looked up with a start.

Colton had approached the driver's side. He was the first to see Craig's face as the young man looked up from the deep study and Colton involuntarily took a step back.

Then the young man looked immediately down.

'Run, run for your life,' came the words of years ago, when, as a boy, he had been walking down a country lane opposite an old, abandoned, rundown house. As a boy, he had run for his life, knowing he was in danger.

The same words came to him now.

But as a man, he could not run, nor would he.

But he was shaken. Why would the same feelings and even the same words come to mind? The look the young man gave Colton made almost made his blood run cold. He had not even seen such a look in the eyes of even the most hardened of criminals he had arrested.

It was the look of a reptile ready to strike, the look of a lion stalking its prey, the look of evil ready to destroy good. It contained the cold emptiness Colton had experienced six years ago.

Impossible.

But in a split second the look was gone, and the young man was smiling up at him.

"Help you, gentlemen?" he asked.

At the same time, Abby exclaimed, "Dad! What are you doing here?"

"Dad?" Craig asked, pretending to look startled. As far as Abby was concerned, he did not know her dad.

Colton was still looking straight at the young man. He knew he had not imagined the words or the feelings he had a few seconds before. He now saw a look of anger pass over the young man's face, but the anger did not seem to be directed at the two men. The anger seemed to be directed inward, as if Craig were mad at himself.

"Dad?" Abby asked again, bringing Colton out of his trance to look at her.

This time he looked at her as a stranger would and was shocked at what he saw.

"Would you come with me, please, Abby?" he asked gently, not willing to use force unless he had to.

"Why? What's wrong?" she asked. "Craig and I were just sitting here talking."

"I know, but I had to find you because of your mother," he said, lying. He didn't care. He wanted her out of the car, out of the physical and emotional reach of the…person?…beside her.

"Mom?" Abby echoed, getting out of her side of the car. Pete had opened the door for her.

"What's wrong with Mom?" she asked, looking scared. "Did she have a wreck or something?"

"Just come on, and you'll see," he said, leading her toward the car.

She looked back at Craig, who nodded to her. Colton

got the impression she was asking for the young man's permission to go with her own dad, for God's sake.

"What? Please tell me," she said as she sucked on one of the orange candy sticks.

As he pulled from the curb, Colton locked her door from his side. Why he was taking such drastic measures, he wasn't sure, only that he felt them necessary. He had the sneaking suspicion she would try to get out of the car, back to Craig, when he admitted there was nothing wrong with her mother, that he only wanted her away from the boy.

He was right, and that made him angry with her.

When he started explaining what he had heard from Mr. Myers and that she was now grounded until her grades came back up, until she attended her meetings and cheerleading practice, she did reach over and try the handle of the door when they came to a stop at an intersection.

She looked so desperate, so haggard in her desperation to try to get back to the boy that Colton started believing what he didn't really want to face.

He felt sick.

Physically ill.

It was not only the bad feeling still sitting like a dozen green apples in the pit of his stomach, but now his anguish came from within.

How could his beautiful, intelligent daughter get hooked in such a short time? How? But more importantly, the question was why. She knew better. He knew she would not knowingly and openly start using drugs.

Then how?

And then not only how, but who. And when he found the person responsible…he couldn't think about what he would do. He didn't want to think about it. He feared his own feelings.

Craig.

Obviously, this Craig was dealing and pushing. He would not be making them, but, certainly, he was dealing.

Just then they pulled into a driveway. Abby recognized their house. She had only just now looked up as they slowed down and turned. She had been too busy opening more of the orange candy to pay attention to where he was driving.

He had furtively been watching her claw around in her purse, desperately searching for more of the candy. She had pushed aside several of the sticks that looked new, rejecting those and, apparently, looking for certain ones.

Chapter 15

They were silent on the way home and as they entered the house. There didn't seem to be anything to say.

When Abby reached the top of the stairs, she turned, feeling her father's eyes on her. She looked down at him, wanting to tell him more about Craig. She was afraid to.

She silently cried out to him for help.

As if he heard her, he started up the stairs.

"Abby," he said.

He had only taken a few steps when she whirled and quickly stepped into her room, practically slamming the door in her haste to get away from him. What was it about his presence that disturbed her so much?

Colton hesitated. He had sensed her cry for help even though she had not said a word. Her face had revealed her despair, a need for help of some kind.

He shut his eyes, willing himself to think of Abby. Although he had not been in there for some time, he pictured her room. He saw her dresser, the white French Provincial piece that matched the canopy bed and study desk. Snapshots of friends and events were stuck into the mirror all around, and the surface of the dresser was cluttered with lipsticks and perfumes. A letter she had received from a friend she had met last summer at camp was open on the dresser.

He pictured all the posters of her favorite singers on her walls, the one of Queen and another of U2, two of her favorite groups. A poster from the movie *Saturday Night Fever* with John Travolta had a prominent spot on one wall. At least these things were there the last time he had been in there. Other songs and groups had come and maybe gone. Maybe other posters were there by now. He finally focused on her and looked on her face as she had turned.

Leaning with her back and the palms of her hands against the door, head hung forward, Abby felt her dad still near.

So, he had sensed she had a problem.

Big deal.

Parents always seemed to know when things were going on in the lives of their kids. Teen-agers could never quite figure out how parents knew such things.

She was tempted to tell him all about Craig.

She turned around and put her hand on the doorknob. Still, she hesitated. He didn't know Craig. The brief encounter he had with him this evening at the park would make Craig so angry that he would surely take it out on her tomorrow. As tough as her dad was, she believed Craig's threat that if she mentioned the candy to anyone, something would happen to her dad and perhaps to her mom, too. It wasn't just the things Craig said. She also sensed a terrible evil within him.

She hadn't felt anything wrong with him at first, but little by little a black emptiness within him had been revealed to her. She knew it was not his intention that she sensed this aberration within him, but she could. She tried not to think about it.

He had slapped her once. It had completely taken her by surprise. No one had ever laid a hand on her, not even her parents. Discipline from them had come in other forms. They did not believe in physically reprimanding children.

She had responded positively to such rearing, never giving them any trouble at all. Not until now. And now she knew what was happening, but she didn't know what to do about it. The helpless feeling was slowing killing her. She was no longer in control of her life. Craig was in control now.

Craig and the orange candy.

That thought frightened her so much that she trembled. She ran to her bed and threw herself on it, crying. The need for the candy was also becoming a raging fire within her. Part of Craig's display of cruelty was in such acts. He told her he would not give her anymore of the candy, that it was up to her to find the one she had lost earlier that day and that would hold her through the night. But it couldn't be found.

She trembled, hurting.

❧

Although Colton had stopped when Abby turned abruptly, he frowned when the door slammed shut. At least he heard it as a slam.

He not only saw it as a slam of a door, but the act itself was shutting him out of her life.

That he refused to accept.

He paused only a few seconds more before starting to climb the stairs to the second floor. Whatever it took, he was going to find out the problem. He would talk to her all night, if necessary.

Marsha came to stand at the bottom of the stairs. She

looked up at Colton. He put his fingers to his lips, signaling her to be quiet and stay downstairs. Using sign language, he told her he was going to talk with Abby.

She nodded her understanding. Marsha had noticed the change in Abby, especially this last week. She and Colton just had not had an opportunity to talk about it.

Maybe he could get Abby to tell him what the problem was. Marsha suspected it was boyfriend trouble, but since father and daughter had a special bond, she was content to let Colton handle it.

Now he hesitated when he reached Abby's door, even when he raised his fist to tap on the door. They never entered each other's room when the door was closed. She had been taught to respect the privacy of others.

But he did rap—twice.

"Abby? Abby, it's me. Dad."

That sounded stupid, even to his ears. Of course, she would know it was him.

"May I come in? I think we need to talk. It's okay, you know."

"No, no, it isn't okay," she nearly screamed, startling him.

It wasn't like Abby to respond like that, even in disagreement. But what was like Abby these days? She was like a different person, not her old self at all.

The old Abby was a very soft-spoken person, hardly ever raising her voice at all to others, even though he knew she was capable of it. That fact was evident in her cheering. She had a clear, strong, loud voice when cheering her team on to victory.

Now that same voice was threatening to keep him out of her life.

"Let me in and let's talk about it. Let me help, pumpkin."

He used another favorite name for her.

Pumpkin?

Pumpkins were orange, weren't they?

"Keep out," Abby almost screamed again. Then it was almost as if she just as quickly changed her mind. She threw her door open, facing him. She had a tear-stained face. Her eyes were already red from crying. "Dad? Do you remember earlier when we were talking in the kitchen?"

"Talking? Is that what you call it?"

She frowned but did not answer his comment.

Stupid, he told himself. *Don't say anything else stupid like that to make her clam up.*

"Dad, after I left, did you find one of my orange candy sticks in the kitchen? It must have fallen out of my purse."

Colton was startled. He wasn't sure what he had expected her to say but it certainly wasn't this. She opened the door for him just to ask him about that orange candy? No other reason?

"Abby, we need to talk about some things—"

"You're always needing to talk, Dad," she interrupted. "About the candy—"

He shook his head. He was convinced.

First Jack.

Now this.

What next?

"I really don't remember, Abby. I thought you picked all those up and put them in your purse."

His voice had just the right hesitation and question to it.

"I was missing one," she said.

"So?" he asked. He shrugged, pretending indifference. "Just go buy some more tomorrow."

"You don't understand," she said.

She was still standing in the open doorway with Colton still on the second-floor landing. He was struck again by her emaciated figure. She looked like a skeleton standing there with the light behind her.

They stood there and looked at each other for several long seconds. The house was unnaturally silent.

"Oh, Daddy," she cried. She took two quick steps and practically threw herself into his arms.

He led her into her room and sat down with her on the side of the bed. She broke down, crying, her body jerking as he held her. He stroked her hair as she cried.

How tiny she felt in his arms. She stopped crying and leaned back from him. She would not look at him.

"Abby, look at me," he said, softly, reaching out to put his hand under her chin.

She hesitated then allowed her head to be tilted up, so she looked at him.

"Tell me," he said, simply.

"I can't," she whispered, shaking her head.

Stay calm, Colton told himself. "Whatever it is, no matter what it is, you can tell me. You know that, don't you, sweetheart?"

She nodded, agreeing. She had always been able to talk to her dad. He was the one she had gone to with problems over the years instead of her mother.

Colton waited patiently.

She looked up at him. "It's him," she began then gasped. "Oh," she cried, as she grabbed her stomach.

"Baby, what's wrong?" Colton asked, scared. "What's happening?"

"It's him," she whispered, getting her breath back. "Somehow he hurts me when I do something he doesn't like. I don't know how he does it, just like I don't know how he knows what I'm doing or saying, but somehow, he does know. He said he'd hurt you, too—oh," she cried, again grabbing her stomach. She was in pain.

Intimidation and manipulation might be nebulous things that really could not be touched, but this was real physical pain. Colton could see it on Abby's face.

Craig.

The name came to him, and he knew that was who Abby meant.

What kind of emotional hype had he laid on her?

Voodoo? Hypnotism?

"Lie down," he said, easing her back on the bed.

"Don't go, don't leave me, Daddy," Abby said, grabbing his arm. She had a death grip on him, not letting go of his arm.

"I'm not, baby, I'm staying right here. But be quiet and still and let me concentrate, okay?"

She relaxed, lying back and getting still.

He pulled a chair next to the bed and sat down. "It's okay, honey," he said. "Mom will stay in your bedroom with you tonight, sleep in your bed with you, and stay home with you tomorrow. Be strong, pumpkin, and we'll win. I'm stronger than he is, and we're certainly stronger together, don't you think?"

She nodded.

"How long has he been giving you the orange candy, honey?" he asked gently.

Her eyes opened wide. She wasn't aware that he knew about the candy. How did he know?

"I know, Abby. It isn't candy, and we both know it."

"But I didn't know it, at first, Daddy, honest. Really, it was just a cute game. Then it got where I needed it. But I can quit, I know I can."

"Yes, I know you can, too, sweetheart. But you know you'll have to be strong, don't you? He'll try to overpower you, especially mentally. You must resist, from the very beginning."

She put her hand on her chest. "He was so cute,

Daddy, the new kid at school. Everyone thought he was so cool, and when he seemed to want me, that was wonderful. All the other girls were really jealous. He wanted me."

"I understand," Colton said.

"They don't know who he really is," she said, looking at him, pleading with him to understand. "But I know I can quit."

"Yes, I know you can, too, sweetheart. But you know you'll have to be strong, don't you? You must never be alone. You will have to always have several of your friends around you. Tell them what's happened to you and ask them to help you. *Let* them help you. You know they will."

She nodded. "They don't know what he's really like," she said. "The first week with him was great, just perfect. Then things started moving fast. After that first week, he started saying, 'I love you.' It was pretty stupid of me to believe him, wasn't it?"

"No, honey, not at all. We all believe what we want to believe."

"I know. But when he wanted me to be with him, just him, all the time, I should have suspected something. He didn't want me out of his sight. He said he always wanted to be able to reach out and touch me. Whenever we're in his car, he wants me right next to him or even on his lap when we're stopped or out somewhere. Sometimes it gets embarrassing. I'm with him to the point that I'm no longer with any of my friends anymore. They still try to see me and be with me, especially Sarah, but then Craig is always right there, whisking me away from them. "I took his jealousy of my time and friends as being his love for me. But then—then—"

She couldn't go on. She put her head into her hands. She took a deep breath, willing herself not to cry.

"What then?" he coaxed.

"He—he—slapped me," she sobbed.

"What?" he repeated.

Against his will, his voice rose.

"Now, Dad, don't wig out. Please. He told me I deserved it by going out with Sarah and Amy to the mall when I knew he wanted to be with me. He convinced me, Daddy, that it was my fault. It wasn't, was it? What harm was there in shopping with my two best friends?"

He stroked her hair as her head rested on his shoulder. "Of course, it wasn't your fault, honey. Why didn't you tell me?"

"I couldn't. I just couldn't. I knew you'd want to kill him for it. When he wasn't in one of his moods, he was so cool, Dad."

"Did you tell Sarah or Amy, or somebody, about it?"

"No," she admitted. Her voice was barely audible. "They still thought he was so cool and how lucky I was to be dating him. And, by then, he was giving me the candy, and I needed it from him. Sarah and Amy, and especially Sarah, would have started bitching at me to break up with him, and I just couldn't do that. Don't you understand that?"

"Yes, I understand," he said. This peer pressure business could sometimes be carried too far.

"And I couldn't tell you or Mom because you've always trusted me to make good decisions. You've told me how good my judgment is, and I didn't want to disappoint you. I certainly didn't want to be grounded or anything like that. Not with the Winter Dance coming up.

"But you did see that slapping you was wrong, didn't you?" he asked.

They had talked about such behavior while dating being unacceptable. Had she forgotten?

"Yes, but I didn't see one slap as a problem. I just

thought his possessiveness was part of his love for me. And he could be so much fun most of the time."

Her eyes begged him to understand. He did understand. It just angered him, that's all.

"And everybody thought we had the perfect relationship. They thought we were the perfect pair. I didn't want to tell anyone that he slapped me because then they might blame me for it or something. I really don't know what I thought. I just didn't want to look bad in front of my friends."

"I know. Did he ever slap you again?"

She hesitated, but she knew it was no use lying to her dad. He would get the truth out of her sooner or later. It was his business to get hardened criminals to confess. She didn't stand a chance and she knew it. "Yes," she confessed. "And he would grab my arms and squeeze real hard sometimes. See."

She pushed up her sleeve on one arm. He could see bruises around her arm in the shape of fingerprints.

His anger had been increasing as she talked. Now it hit a real high. "That's it," he said, standing up. "That guy is history."

"Dad, please," Abby begged, standing up beside him and putting her hand on his arm. "Don't do anything rash. Please. I know what's going on now. I can beat this thing. We can beat him."

He was breathing hard. He could hardly contain his anger at the young man. He willed himself to calm down.

"I'll get your mom," he said. "Why don't you stay home from school tomorrow? Your mom can take a day off and stay with you. It will be a beginning. Let him start wondering about you."

"Dad?"

Colton turned back.

"Thanks for being here for me. I need you. I love

you. Thanks for not being mad at me for messing up my life like this."

She sounded so young, so helpless.

"I could never be mad at you, Abby. This is nothing you've done. You have no reason to feel guilty. You didn't make the choice to begin with. Now, you can."

She nodded and laid her head back on the pillow, closing her eyes. "You're okay with this?" she asked.

"What?"

"He said if I told anyone about the candy or didn't do what he said, he said—he said he could kill you."

Colton's anger returned. He held it in check for Abby's sake. He didn't want her to think for even a second that he was mad at her or blamed her for any of this. He clenched his fists as his side, thankful for the subdued lighting in the room. "No way. *That* you must believe. Do you have faith in me?"

"Yes, always. But I had forgotten. Don't be mad."

"I'm not, pumpkin. I'm not angry with you at all. Just at myself for not seeing your problem sooner, before now. Will you forgive me for not realizing sooner that something was wrong? I will never again get too involved in my work to overlook what's happening to you."

"Of course, Daddy, but..." She paused, not sure what to say, but needing to ask something, anyway.

"What?"

"W—What are you going to do? About Craig, I mean? Arrest him for possession?"

"We'll try, but if he sees he can't get to you anymore, we'll never catch him with anything but candy."

Abby suddenly gave a short laugh. "It's funny, isn't it? There I was so anti-drug everything. I was so proud that the drug scene never affected me. It just goes to show, doesn't it? Never say 'never.' Right, Dad? I really have a lot to explain to my friends. And others," she added. "But it's never too late, is it?"

"No, honey, it isn't. But…" This time it was his turn to pause. He didn't want to say the wrong thing to burst her newfound bubble. But he knew they had not even come to the worst part yet, much less having put anything behind them.

"What?" she asked, in the same way he had questioned her a few minutes ago.

"It's far from over, sweetheart. This Craig probably has someone else behind him and that someone is not going to give up on you, and he's not going to let Craig stop, either. They will try to find a way to get to you."

"I know, Daddy, but now I'm back to myself again. I just won't be alone, ever, like you said. I'll tell my friends, and they'll all stay around me. Physically, I mean. Literally. He won't be able to touch me."

"But you must be prepared for him to try. Yes, you're stronger because you've recognized your problem. But, please, don't ever, ever underestimate him. It could be your downfall. Don't ever think you're too strong, okay?"

She nodded.

Colton knew she felt things were okay now, but he wasn't so sure. They had a long way to go.

Chapter 16

He willed himself to relax, putting all thoughts toward this Craig, wherever he might be. He knew he could touch him.

For a minute, there was nothing. Then Colton touched on such coldness, emptiness, that he nearly recalled his thoughts. He likened it to touching a hot stove and immediately drawing your hand back.

He willed himself to reach out again, to seek out this emptiness, because he knew that was Craig.

And he knew there was something about Craig that made him less, or perhaps more, than human. Colton had felt him before, and he knew.

He also knew that Craig was doing all he could to block Colton's thoughts from seeking him out.

Colton sent his thoughts to Craig. *'I'm going to get you. You are not going to get me or Abby. I will seek you out until I find you, and I will kill you.'*

What startled him the most was the fact that the *source* of that rage and hatred was a lot closer than Colton had hoped.

This would not be easy, Colton knew. Also, he knew, others would probably die before it was over.

He shook his head, breaking the contact. He reached out and touched Abby, who was still trembling.

He felt her agreement.

But he also felt the fear of Craig she still possessed.

Chapter 17

Dan! Hey, what a surprise. Since you just called last week, I wasn't expecting to hear from you for a while now. What's happening?"

Colton had answered the phone, once again expecting it to be the precinct telling him there was still another murder.

He either expected to hear from the office or maybe one of Abby's teachers with something else she wasn't doing these days.

"Well…ll…" said Dan, drawing out the word. "You really won't believe this, you really won't. Guess what?"

"I'll bite. What?" Colton asked. What could it be?

Dan was his twin brother from Arkansas. They had met six years ago when Colton was on vacation to his hometown.

Neither had known the other existed. Dan, a local county sheriff, had helped Colton solve the mystery that just saved Abby's life "in the nick of time," so to speak. In fact, despite Colton's apparent bravery and thoughts of going it alone, he would not have been able to rescue Abby if Dan had not been there to help him. They had to kill the abductor/murderer at the time. There had been no other choice. From that point on, they had become and remained good friends.

"I assume you've heard of the proverbial 'deathbed confession'?" Dan asked.

"Sure, who hasn't? But in our business, you know it rarely happens. Most of these turkeys just take whatever they know to the grave with them, unless, of course, they want to get even with someone. Then, they might spill their guts. But, what's up? Someone we know make a deathbed confession?"

"You might say that. I heard about it in a round-about way. I thought you would be interested in knowing about it, too."

Dan paused. Colton knew his brother was keeping him in suspense on purpose. "Okay, big guy. Let's have it," Colton responded.

"Well, you remember when you were down here six years ago. Remember Otis Ledbetter?"

Otis? Of course, Colton remembered Otis. How could he forget? Otis had been accused, and even arrested by Dan, of the kidnappings that had taken place over a twenty-year span of time. All of the victims, both young girls and boys, had never been heard of again, although they did find the bones of some of them. Otis had been innocent, though, as Colton and Dan had proved.

"You can't try to tell me that Otis made some kind of confession. He was deaf, as well as developmentally dis-advantaged, if I remember, and couldn't even write."

"No, I'm not going to try to tell you Otis did. Re-member Tom, Otis's friend who helped him all the time?"

"Yes?" Colton answered. He really was starting to get curious. He wondered where all this was leading. He thought they had proved 'whodunit' and said as much to Dan.

"I know. We did. That's not all the story, though. Are you ready for page two?"

"Yes, yes, just get on with it. You know I'm dying to know. Quit stalling."

Dan chuckled, which made Colton smile into the phone.

"Next. You, of course, remember Old Man Ogden?"

Of course, he also remembered Old Man Ogden. This local character had been a definite catalyst in spurring Colton on to locate the culprit.

"Didn't he pass away?" Colton asked. "Did he finally tell all?"

"Actually, he passed away about six months after you went back home. Now, you really need to keep up with this next part. It seems that before he died, he did tell all to someone, and someone else heard the conversation and *that* someone is the one who recently made a deathbed confession. He kept the whole thing more of a secret than Ogden ever did. Guess who?"

Colton made a noise that could almost be considered a growl.

"If you don't hurry up and tell me, I'm going to strangle you over this line."

"Okay, okay. I was just building up a little suspense for you, so you would appreciate this moment."

"I appreciate it. I really do. Now tell me."

"It seems that Tom, Otis's friend, had a good long talk with the old man just a month or so after we solved the *problem*, if you don't mind my putting it that way—" He paused again.

"So, Tom made a confession, did he?" Colton asked, thinking that was obvious.

"No, I heard that Tom was killed in a car accident about a year ago."

Colton really was beginning to wonder where all this

was leading. If Otis, Ogden, or Tom had not confessed to knowing something about those crimes, then who was left? Those had been the major players, not counting the actual kidnapper/murderer they had killed at the time.

"Thinking further with me, do you remember Adams, the owner of the general store there in Midland?"

"Dan, you're forgetting I'm the one who grew up in Midland. Of course, I remember Adams, clear from the time I was a kid there. Are you getting ready to tell me he confessed to the crimes?"

"No, he really wasn't involved in the murders at all." Dan sensed that now was not the time to stall any longer. Colton needed to know. "According to Adams, Tom went to Ogden about a month after you left. You know how things get around, especially in small towns like that. Tom had 'heard' that Ogden knew everything and there was a possibility he hadn't told everything, certainly not to a stranger. Tom wanted to find out everything Ogden knew."

"So, how did Adams find out all this? Was he in on the conversation, or what?" Colton asked.

"Seems he had just stepped into the storeroom when Tom started asking the old man questions. Guess they thought he was way in the back of the store or something. According to the story, he had paused just inside the storeroom right by the door. He heard most of what was said until a customer came in, called for him, and he had to go to the customer. But, evidently, he heard enough to know what Ogden had never told anyone else."

"And we're to believe that he never told anyone else what he heard all this time?"

Colton was skeptical. This was starting to sound like the usual rumors and stories that go around after something like that happened.

Everybody and his dog in a small town like that had

a theory about what happened and who done it and who it happened to.

"That's the amazing thing, of course. It seems he did keep it a secret. Why? Nobody knows. Now, of course, nobody will ever know. Evidently, though, he had it on his mind the whole time and felt guilty enough about what he knew that he told it when he knew he was dying. As I heard it, it wasn't in his last few seconds or anything like that. He told it to a nephew about two days before he passed away. I've heard of people doing that, confessing to things at their death. I guess it makes their last few days or moments of dying easier. It seems to me, though, it might just leave more sorrow and sadness for those still living. What do you think?"

"I think you've been had, brother," Colton said.

"No, honestly, this came from a very reliable source," Dan insisted.

"Okay, you know the people there. So, what did he say?"

"Well, you won't believe this, you really won't."

Colton was starting to grin. "Okay, I promise I won't believe it, but why don't you tell me anyway?"

"Here goes. We know that Otis and Tom were twins, right?"

"Reasonably sure, right," Colton agreed.

"Well, Old Man Ogden told Tom that Granny Spenser knew there was something in the basement of their old house and finally went crazy with the knowledge. She had even fed whatever was in the basement from time to time."

Colton drew in his breath sharply. What was this?

"It seems Granny Spenser started talking to Old Man Ogden about the 'evil' in her basement. Now, Ogden loved Granny, had since they were children, so he humored her for years and years. It was only after little boys and girls started disappearing that he finally decided there might be something to her ramblings."

"And what about Tom?"

"He knew."

"Yes, you said Tom knew. Knew what? But what happened?"

"Tom sometimes watched Otis for the mother whenever she needed to go to town for something and could not take Otis. Remember, their place was just the next one down the road from Otis. It seems that Tom confessed to seeing the same thing that Otis saw, the boys and girls disappearing down Spenser's Lane and never returning. But he didn't tell anyone about seeing them. He didn't want anyone to think it was him. I think he must have been starting to go a little crazy at that time, certainly paranoid. It was Tom, that's what I mean. Tom started talking about aliens and things coming to earth from space. People were starting to think he was going crazy."

Colton was silent. He really wasn't sure he was getting all this.

"And maybe, just maybe, that's why Tom always felt a need to help and befriend Otis. Maybe he was drawn to him for that reason, that he knew there was something there all along and never spoke up about it."

"Have you talked to Tom's widow about this?" Colton asked.

"I tried to," Dan said. "I drove down there as soon as I heard this story. It seems that she moved away about a year ago. I asked several people in the town if they knew where she had moved to, but no one did. There was one older lady who liked to talk a lot who told me she thought Tom's wife had family in West Virginia, but there's no one to verify that. They had a child that left with the wife, of course."

"Are you sure about the child?" Colton asked.

He could almost see Dan shrug.

"That's what I heard. I went out to Tom's place. It had been bought, but the new owners didn't know where she was, either. Tom had been a shade-tree mechanic. People brought their cars to his place, and he fixed them in his own yard and driveway. The new owners had tried to find her because she had promised to remove several old junker car bodies and parts from around the place but never did. They finally gave up trying to find her and hauled the old cars off themselves.

"That's another reason why Tom probably never had a birth certificate. He worked out of his own yard, probably took pay in cash or food, so he never needed a Social Security card to work anywhere. Probably paid any doctors' visits in cash."

"Post office?" Colton asked.

Dan knew what he meant. "I checked. Tom's widow had rented a box for a while, but closed it about a month after the sale of the place went through. They didn't have a forwarding address on her."

"You think she wanted to deliberately disappear for some reason?" Colton asked.

"If she did, only she knows the reasons," Dan replied, "but disappear she did. Of course, I've got a theory about that."

"Which is…" Dan prompted.

"These people down here can be funny in some ways. It Tom's widow thought everyone in town was looking at him because he knew something about the kidnapper/murderer of the little girls, she probably felt shame and embarrassment. It might even have caused his mechanic business to fall off to the point he couldn't support his family there. People here worry about what their neighbors think. Sometimes they think the actions of their relatives reflect on them, thinking the neighbors might blame them."

"Funny way to look at things."

"Yes, but still a fact."

"Why would Tom think anyone else knew about him? If he thought Adams was far enough away to not be able to hear him and Ogden, why would he think anyone else knew?"

Colton could almost see Dan shrug at the other end of the line.

"Maybe he worried that if Ogden were so willing to tell him, maybe he would tell others. Ogden did rattle on sometimes, you know."

Colton laughed.

"How well I know. At the time, it was hard to know which part of what he was saying was real and what was his imagination."

"At least you picked enough of the truth out of what he said to save Abby," Dan said.

"You're right about that. At least I owe him that. I like fairy tales. Can you get more details for me about this? Just check everywhere. Also, would you make doubly sure that Tom is dead? Find out everything you can about the wreck?"

"What're you thinking?" Dan asked.

"I'm not sure," Colton replied. "It's just one of those feelings I have. Felt it coming on as soon as you started talking. Just do the checking, okay? By the way, who's taking care of Otis now?"

"He's in the local institution here in Fort Smith."

"Ouch," Colton said.

"Yeah, I know. But you know how it is even with families nowadays. How can you expect anyone to take care of someone like Otis when it's not even family? I saw him once. He just sits there in his room, rocking back and forth.”

“No rabbits anywhere?”

“No, they don’t allow pets.”

“Too bad.”

“And, Colton, there is something more I need to tell you.”

“Now, what? It seems the clues on this case, or cases, seem to be piling up, with more and more surprises.”

“This is not about the case you’re working on there in Denver. This is something personal.”

“Oh?” asked Colton.

“Are you sitting down?”

Colton sighed. Dan had always had a knack for the dramatic. He wondered what this could be.

“Sure,” he answered.

“I had a conversation with my Uncle George.”

He related the conversation to Colton, almost word for word…

Chapter 18

Six years earlier:

"Oh, Dan—" began his uncle.

Dan blinked. His uncle's voice told him there was something he needed to know.

"About this Granny Spenser thing. Don't be too quick to dismiss it as a lot of superstitious garbage. People believed in her. We, the family, I mean, believed in her, and everyone believed her. There was *always* one in each generation who had 'The Sight.' Since it's obviously not been one of mine or Seth's children, we thought maybe you—"

He didn't finish his sentence or thought.

He's hoping I can finish for him, Dan thought. *He's hoping I can tell him I have this special witchy gift or something.* "Sorry to disappoint you, Uncle George, but I don't seem to have a special ability of this kind. So, I guess that means it's going to skip a generation here."

George could tell by the tone of his voice that Dan didn't believe him.

"Actually, there could be another possibility," responded George.

"What do you mean?" asked Dan.

"Well, you know your mother came back to us after being away for several years. She came back one winter night, you in her arms, just about three months old. She only had a small paper bag of clothes with her. Of course, your grandmother and grandfather took her right back in. Dan, your mother was the one in our generation who had 'The Sight.' She never wanted to admit it, made fun of it. She always got up and left the room if someone started talking about it. But you know all this, don't you?"

"Yes," answered Dan. He knew about his mother, who had run away from home, but brought her baby back—him—when she got sick and could not provide for herself of her baby.

"You know she was very, very ill, and died shortly after coming back to us. What you've never been told is that while she was feverish, she kept saying things like 'where's my baby?' and 'they took my baby' and 'I want my baby back.' We thought at the time, of course, that she was always referring to you, and we would bring you to her, put you in her arms. That seemed to quiet her some, but she still raved on about her baby that was gone.

"It was only after she passed away that we began wondering if, perhaps, there was another child some-where. We investigated. We located one place she had lived after you were born, and one old lady in the apartment building said she sometimes saw your mother with two babies, but after several weeks, there was only one, so she thought she was just babysitting, or something. She forgot all about it. The neighbor remembered Hazel getting ill, though, and she's the one who talked her into going 'home.' And we're glad she did, of course, not only because we had you to raise, but we had our beautiful sister back with us, if only for a little while. She never was able to tell us why she left town so suddenly. She stayed too ill until the day she died. But we loved her all we could, you know. Before and after she left."

"Yes, I know, Uncle George," Dan agreed. But what was he trying to tell him now? Was he trying to say that he could have a brother or sister somewhere?

"You're telling me I could have a brother or sister, aren't you? And that this brother or sister could be the one with Granny's power. Is that it?"

Dan could almost see George shrug his shoulders on the other end of the line.

"Just a guess," he said. "But I suppose we'll never know."

⁊⊙⁊⊙

Present Day:

"That was the end of the conversation," said Dan.

Colton was stunned.

Did he have "The Sight?" Was this why he always had "feelings" about things, could almost sense things before they were going to happen—even after they had happened, what *had* happened?

"Colton, are you there? Have I lost you? Do you understand what I am saying?"

"Oh, yes, I understand what you are saying. It's just incredible, that's all. I can't believe it. I've always known I had some sort of special ability. I've even been teased by the guys on the force, both in Chicago and here, about being 'psychic.' In fact, sometimes I don't tell things I seem to know about a case for fear someone might think I know *too* much about it and accuse me of being involved. This is amazing!"

"Isn't it? I didn't tell Uncle George about you. I didn't think you would want any more notoriety in that area with this case you are working on."

"Thanks for that," said Colton. "You're right, there. I'm probably going to have to do some investigating on my own about these cases, rather than let too many know what I'm thinking about and putting together."

Colton really could not take in what he had just heard from Dan. But he knew it was the truth.

He felt it.

"Yeah," Dan said. "Look, give me a couple, three days and I'll give you a call back, okay?"

"Great. Thanks for calling."

Colton hung up the phone with a chuckle.

What a tale.

But he had a funny feeling about it.

Colton didn't believe in coincidences. Too many years on the force and too many cases with too many clues had convinced him there was no such thing.

Was Dan's call a warning?

A clue?

A premonition?

Chapter 19

Colton was back in his office. He reached over and picked up the reports about the homeless drug victims.

Drug toxicity Jack had written as the cause of death on each. Something about the reports still bothered him, especially in light of the facts Jack had discovered.

His mind was going over and over the locations of the deaths. He tossed the papers he held onto his desk. From his position, he could see a large wall map of the City and County of Denver on the wall of the precinct room. The City and County were the same.

He started at the location on the map where the first body had been found. It had been found near Federal Boulevard and West Moncrief Avenue. Yeah, he granted, that was a good place to find a homeless druggie. He pointed in the air, spotting that location with his finger.

Logical.

He leaned over and picked up the papers, shuffling them to find the second report. The second OD was just at the south end of the Denver Stockyards at the viaduct over the Platte River near the Amtrak line. Again, that was a logical place for a homeless drug addict to be. Most of Denver's homeless "lived" in the viaducts, especially those of the Platte River. This second one was about three miles away from the first in a different area of town. Yet, in a way, they were alike.

Again, he pinpointed the location by putting his finger on the map in the air.

One man poked his head in the door.

"You okay?" he asked, grinning.

Colton smiled back. "Just thinking about the map. You know how that goes," he replied.

"Yeah, all too well."

The man withdrew.

Now, where was that next one? The third OD took place between Dexter and Cherry Streets on Martin Luther King, Jr. Boulevard Parkway. Again, this was still a logical place for a homeless druggie to have connected with a pusher, got some bad dope and OD'd. Still, nothing was evident to set up a red flag and draw attention to these deaths.

To anyone else, there was nothing to connect them. Just knowing about the orange-tinted tissue was driving him crazy. He knew the connection was there. He just had to find it.

The sixth one. He looked at the report then up at the map. Near East Colfax and Jersey Streets.

Still a drug area.

Still logical for an overdose.

Still logical for homeless.

Again, the finger in the air. He went from the first to the second to the sixth. Still, he saw no connection. They were basically different parts of Denver. The only similarity was that each of these areas was logical for homeless, drugs, and ODs.

Where did the fifth happen? Oh, Glendale. Near Birch and Kentucky Streets. He nodded. The community of Glendale had changed drastically in the last five to six years. Some apartment managers blamed it on the fact that in the early '80s Denver hit an economic slump. People had moved away from Denver. To survive in some areas, management companies had to lower lease rates and deposit requirements at their apartment complexes in order to maintain a decent occupancy rate.

This, of course, attracted lower income tenants. When the economy started booming again, and people started moving back to Denver, this left those apartments still lower income. Higher-salaried citizens did not choose to move there. Without the higher rents and resources to provide adequate maintenance, some of this housing had gradually become rundown. Some companies raised their rents again, forcing tenants out. But some, it seemed, had given up on their investment.

The western part of Glendale was funny. From one block to the next you had rundown housing and expensive new apartments with exclusive office buildings in-between.

But drug dealers had moved in, and this fifth death was a result of a changing environment there.

But still logical.

He closed his eyes and shook his head. He leaned back in his chair. He rubbed the back of his neck with a hand. Maybe he needed a break from all this. But how did you take a break from life? Or from death?

The sixth.

Where?

Buchtel and East Florida. The body had been spotted in the high grass on the slope near the I-25 overpass. A man had been walking his dog one morning when the dog pulled on the leash and started barking at something. Since the dog didn't bark that often, the man had investigated and found the body.

Colton frowned. This one didn't make sense. This was a different type of neighborhood. It was a better socio-economic part of town than where the other deaths had taken place. Homes in this area were moderately upscale, older but with dignity. They were still being bought by upper-middle-income people and were holding their value. There weren't usually any homeless reported in this area.

Ah, here it was. A notation by the investigation officer read "brought to scene?"

That made sense. Of course, it didn't make sense to anyone thinking it was an overdose. Yet, with his training, the officer had realized something was not right about the man's body ending up there.

Who was the officer? Colton nodded. The man was a good, solid policeman with good instincts. "Thank you for that note," Colton said, out loud. He would talk to the man, get his thoughts about the scene.

Again, the finger in the air.

Next?

The seventh OD took place near West Alameda and Clay Streets.

Ah, now we are in the west part of Denver again, he thought. He looked up at the map and located the spot.

This area could make sense for homeless although it had a lesser concentration of homeless or druggies than the others.

Where next? Here it was. Twentieth Street Viaduct at Jason Street near the Platte River. *Oh, good,* he thought sarcastically. *At least we're back in the best part of town for this sort of thing. What is going on here?*

Only once before had Denver had such a rash of murders. Once there had been fifteen homicides in two weeks. Those had been verified homicides. He had to remember that only he thought these were.

His finger in the air spotted the next OD.

South Colorado and Eighth Avenue. Back over there? He frowned. Maybe some homeless there raided the hospital dumpsters for food and found some places to sleep at night. But it just didn't make sense.

These deaths moving from one place to the other just didn't make any sense to him.

"Moving? Did I say moving?" he said out loud.

"Moving. Hmm."

He had an idea. He quickly made a list of the locations on a piece of paper that he could hold up in front of him with one hand as he traced the routes of the deaths with the other. Again, his finger in the air went from the first to the second to the third and so on.

"Well, I'll be damned," he said. "That can't be."

He traced the deaths again. There definitely was a pattern here. Taken in a straight line from one to the other, they made a crude circle.

He opened the bottom drawer of his desk, rummaging around for a smaller city map.

He was excited. He was on to something here. He knew it. He stood up. He unfolded the accordion map and opened it out flat, spreading it over the papers on his desk.

He uncapped a red felt pen. Starting with the first death, he put a large red dot at each site. He took a pencil and connected the dots with a straight line.

"That's it. I knew it."

He took the pencil and connected the dots again, this time curving the lines out as he went from one to the other.

There it was. It was a pattern, and the pattern formed a perfect spiral. Starting with the seventh murder, the spiral had begun its second circle inward. The locations of deaths eight and nine were equal distance from the spiral pattern of deaths one, two, three, six, and five around the circle.

He was stunned. He just stood here staring at the map. He couldn't believe what he knew he was seeing. There was no way this could simply be a coincidence.

These murders were happening in a spiral pattern. He hadn't been wrong thinking there were murders. Someone had a plan here. What the plan was had yet to be figured out.

A spiral.

He saw it so clearly. Didn't a spiral have a center point? If this killer had this pattern going, what was he working toward?

He bent over the map. Taking the same distance between the first and what was not the second ring of the spiral, he projected the spiral to its conclusion.

He stared at the location for a full minute, at least, before he could voice it to himself.

It was his street. In fact, it was his house. Even taking several streets in either direction, the end of the spiral led to him.

To him?

Why?

And who?

Did they really have a methodical psycho on their hands? Were these really just random ODs? But why not? Weren't psychotics very methodical? Didn't they meticulously plan their deeds, even down to the last detail? Wasn't it always the man or woman next door that played with the kids and petted the neighbors' dogs? Wasn't it always who you least expected?

That was one thing he had learned in this business. Never discount the illogical.

He decided it was time to see if others saw the same thing.

He called Pete over.

"Tell me. What is it?" Pete asked.

Colton went to the map on the wall. It was a large map showing the entire Metro Denver area. Red pushpins had been placed on the spots where the ODs had taken place.

They had decided to track them because of the two obvious connections—homeless and overdoses. The department had not yet been willing to say they were being killed for a reason, or no reason, for that matter.

"Now, follow me. Look." He pointed to Federal Boulevard and West Moncrief where the first murder took place. "Now, here is where the second one happened." Again, he pointed with his finger to the spot. "Now, again, there is the third place."

"So? What pattern?" Pete asked. "I don't see a pattern. I see three drug overdoses. What about numbers six, five, six, and seven? What are you seeing that I don't?"

"This," Colton said. He took his finger, beginning with the murder in the Northwest part of the Metro area, murder number one, and went to the second murder. But instead of taking his finger and going in a straight line from one to the other, like from point A to point B, he made his finger swing out in an arch from the first to the second. Then, he did the same thing from the second murder to the third, and so on. "See it yet?" he asked Pete.

"Yeah, I see it, but I don't believe it. You're showing me a circle here."

"No, think further than a circle," Colton said as he continued with his finger, "I'm saying these…deaths …are taking place in a spiral pattern."

Pete was excited. He could see it, now that Colton had shown it to him. Several other men and one woman cop on the shift, Marie, had stopped what they were do-ing and had gathered around Colton.

"Show us that again," one of the said.

Colton showed them.

"Makes sense to me," one of them commented.

"Me, too, but what does it mean?" Marie asked. "I mean, a spiral usually has something in the center of it, doesn't it?"

They all looked at her.

She shrugged. "What I'm thinking of is those little spiral-type puzzles they put on the mini-page for the kids in the newspaper. Something like that. You have to find your way through the maze, which is essentially a basic spiral pattern. Or, say, the squirrel has to find his way to the nut in the center. That's what I was thinking of," she concluded.

"You're right, Marie," Colton agreed, looking back toward the map.

"So, what's in the center of this spiral?" one of them asked, taking a step closer.

What was the middle of this one?

They stood staring at the map for a few moments, trying to figure out the center. They were all trying to decide just exactly what *was* in that part of town.

Pete was the first to respond. "Oh, my God, it couldn't be."

"What?" several asked.

"Keeping the right proportions and then taking this spiral to its logical end, you come to…well…" He turned to look at Colton. "Don't you live someone right here?" he asked as he put his finger on the map.

"Umm…" said Colton, stepping closer.

"Didn't you buy one of those old brownstones in that area? To fix it up?" one of the officers behind him asked. "Isn't that near you, Colton?"

"Yeah, it is."

"But this doesn't make sense," Marie piped up again. "Why or how could ODs be taking place in a spiral and why closing in on Colton? There's no reason for it. Is there?"

She asked the question to silence. No one had an answer to either of her questions.

They all were thinking the same thing. If this really was a pattern they were seeing, then it meant the ODs were no longer random, and they probably were no longer just simple ODs. This meant homicides, and that put everything in a completely different ballpark. And no one really liked to play in that park.

Colton lived in an upscale area of the old part of town. It was called Maple Ridge. There was no rhyme or reason for the name. There were no maples anywhere around it although it had a small greenbelt down the middle of the main row of houses. The developer must have just liked the sound of the name.

Pete located the exact location of the subdivision on the map, making the spiral smaller and smaller as it neared that part of town. There were two isolated cases, or so it had seemed, not far from the station house, one to the west and one to the southwest.

"Abby's school?" Pete asked. Why he was seriously buying into this idea that the deaths were taking place in a spiral, he did not know. Could he really be thinking this way? Could they all? He looked around at his fellow officers. They were still staring at the map seemingly not sure what they wanted to see or believe.

Colton pointed to a street not too far from where he lived. There was a dot near there. "Remember? That was the third body that was found. That was the one where Ric saw something and called us in."

"I don't know," Pete responded. "It is near Abby's

school and near your house." He pointed to two isolated cases on the fringes of the city and looked around the squad room. "But what about these two?"

"I bet if we checked, we would find those were the first two cases," Colton mused. "In fact, I have an idea."

Chapter 20

"Mike," Colton called, and a young man who had put the pins on the map looked their way.

"Sir?" he asked.

Colton motioned for him to come there.

"Take your list and write the number on these circles that I'm going to put beside each of these pins. Put the numbers in chronological order of which death took place when. We want to see where the first one happened, and so on."

"Yes, sir," Mike said.

He quickly located a list and went right to work.

All of them felt a little foolish right now. They did not look at each other but silently watched the young man. Since there were so many drug overdoses and quite a few homicides, no one had thought much about when any of these had taken place. They had simply happened. They were still wondering if they really were seeing a pattern emerging.

When the young man finished, they discovered that Colton was right.

"I suspect with these first two, that the killer was just feeling us out, feeling out the area, getting to know it, trying to determine if he was in the right location, even the right city."

"What do you mean?" one of them asked.

"And do you think the killer has decided he is in the right area?" Pete asked at the same time. *Whatever Colton's starting to believe or wants to believe about this case, at least he's sure he's right*, Pete thought, still watching Colton.

"Suppose this is someone after you, Colton," one of the men asked. "The next question would be who and why, and then the next question would be, why not just stake you out and kill you some night when you came home late? Why is he trying to get all this attention?"

"Killing me quickly is not what he wants to do," Colton responded. "He wants to play with all of us, especially me, make me suffer, then he hopes to destroy me. And he also hoped to throw me off with all these drug killings. They were simply distractions."

"He's playing with us, all right," Marie said. "Just like the arsonist likes to stick around and watch a house burn, so this guy is killing these poor, homeless people to watch Colton squirm."

"You could be right," several agreed.

"Yeah, like the FBI thinking that security guard at the Olympics planted that bomb in Centennial Park then helped move people out of the way before he watched what the bomb did."

"Well, sort of," Colton replied.

"This is certainly an interesting theory we've bought into here, but what if it just ain't so?" one of the veterans on the force asked.

They all turned to look at him.

"Well, if it is so, then Colton has to decide who is after him and why, don't you, Colton?"

They were all silent.

"Yeah, Colton, who did you send to prison that has a cousin who has a brother-in-law that's coming after you for putting Bubba in jail when Bubba was really a good ole boy?"

They all laughed.

"That's a good question," he agreed.

"Well, I for one am going back to my own case. I'm not even sure you guys aren't completely bananas with this one."

One man turned and walked away, and they all decided to scatter. They turned away with comments of "you're on your own with this one, Colton, old man" and "go get 'im, Colton."

Whether any of them agreed or disagreed they knew there was no proof that any of the deaths really were murders or that they really were taking place in a spiral. It could all be coincidental and circumstantial.

They had other jobs to finish.

Colton and Pete looked at each other. They were the only ones still standing in front of the map.

"You think I'm crazy, don't you?" Colton asked Pete. "You think I've decided, just out of the blue, that we're the eventual victims, right?"

Pete shrugged, unable to meet his partner's eyes. He wasn't committing himself to believe anything at this point.

"Let's go get some fresh air," Colton said, reaching for his coat.

When they were seated in a booth in a favorite café down the street, Colton looked across at Pete. "Before you were transferred here and became my partner, something happened that you will not want to believe. It was one of those bizarre cases that most policemen or women just don't ever have to deal with. But what I'm about to tell you is true, and others can tell you it is."

Pete was all ears. He knew how there were some on the force that thought Colton had ESP or was psychic or something. He had witnessed it off and on. He knew something interesting was coming.

He sat riveted to his seat as Colton told him about what had happened in the small town of Midland, Arkansas, six years previously. He was not even aware of the waitress bringing them cup after cup of coffee as Colton told him about his daring rescue of Abby and how the mystery was solved.

"But you haven't heard the most interesting, what I feel is the most important part," Colton continued.

"And what is that?" Pete asked. What else could there be?

"My brother, Dan, called a few nights ago and said he'd heard a story that there had been a deathbed confession by one of the locals, something about aliens and secrets kept over the years about a thing in the basement of an old house that ate the little boys and girls that disappeared."

"Let me get this straight," Pete said, as he went through the story again. "And you think this…whatever it was…that you and Dan killed…might be coming after you now? And Abby? Or, maybe you didn't really kill it or him or whatever?"

Pete had never questioned Colton before, but doubts were setting in.

"No, actually, we killed it."

"Are you sure?" Pete asked. "Sounds like, if you didn't put a wooden stake through its heart, it might be coming after you because you rescued Abby. Can't steal a man's food, you know." His tone said he didn't believe a word of it.

"Pete," was all Colton said. He managed to look hurt.

"Sorry," Pete apologized. "Are you really sure, though, that he was killed?"

"Well, that same thought came to my mind. Dan is doing a thorough investigation of the matter. He's going to call me back in a couple of days now."

"If this Tom is dead, then who could be after you?" Pete asked.

"I don't know. I really don't know," Colton said, quietly.

They were silent as the waitress brought the food they had finally ordered.

"You don't believe in this spiral thing, do you?" Colton finally asked.

"I don't know, I really don't," Pete replied. "I want to, but—"

He didn't finish. What else was there to say?

"I know," Colton said. "It's okay. Lunch is on me, okay?"

"Sure," Pete agreed. "I'll get it next time."

After a few minutes of silence while they ate, Colton had one thing to ask of his partner. "If things get a little crazy and seemingly unbelievable from this point on, will you still help me?" he asked.

Now it was Pete's turn to look hurt. "You have to ask? Of course, I'm loyal to my partner. And my friends."

"Thank you," Colton responded simply.

They were silent for a few minutes, sipping even more coffee.

"But what do you think whoever is doing this will do next? Has he killed enough homeless druggies to get your attention?"

"I'll let him know he has," Colton replied.

"And how will you do that?"

"I'm not sure yet," Colton answered, "but there's got to be a way of finding out who it is."

Chapter 21

Jack leaned back in his chair, stretching his arms high above his head. He had been hunched over the microscope for so long that his shoulders ached. There was a sharp, jabbing pain down one side of his neck.

He had become engrossed in analyzing the chemical composition of this new drug he had discovered. The similarities of the drug in the bodies of the overdose victims had kept him so involved that he had lost all track of time. The aches and cramps that came with the job were momentarily forgotten.

It was long into the night, or the early morning hours, whichever way you wanted to look at it. His wife would have given up long ago and retired to bed. She knew better than to disturb him in the middle of a case. She knew he'd be safe. That's all that mattered.

There was a time when she would have still been up, watching for the glow of every headlight coming around the corner in her direction. That was when Jack had been an active detective on the force, even been on the streets some of the time. That was many, many years ago.

At her insistence, he had gone back to college. She had supported them both financially as she worked diligently as a legal secretary. Emotionally she could leave him alone to study night after night. She had never felt ignored or left out. Curled up with a book on her lap she had been content to sit and read as he "hit the books." Just being in the same room with him had been enough to see them through those times.

Jack had never really enjoyed an active medical practice. He had been more interested in diagnosing than treating. Attention to detail was his forte. That's why he had given up medicine and joined the police force. But now Jack had really found his niche in life.

He was following a specialty in criminology and pathology that naturally led to forensics. Since the love of police work was already flowing through his veins, he had become a pathologist with the force and now headed the forensics department. He was the county medical examiner as well. For some strange reason that he never questioned or tried to explain, he really enjoyed performing autopsies.

He was good. No, he was beyond good. He was superior at his work. There were many cases that had been solved because Jack had detected some minute foreign material and had identified the source. He not only kept up with new advances in his field, he seemed to always be ahead of them.

These nine similar cases, one of which he was working on right now, were attributed to drug overdoses. They could have been a result of a shipment of heroin laced with fentanyl, or other bad drugs. The peculiar orange residue in the tissues of the lips and under the fingernails was still a mystery to him. He had formulated some personal opinions. But, he didn't have enough hard evidence now to present anything to the higher-ups, though. The police department was fully aware of what a false alarm might do to the drug community. The only one he had told was Colton. He had proved to be a good friend both on and off the force. Besides, Colton seemed to have a sixth sense about things.

It would have been simple if it had been new stuff coming up from Mexico or Columbia or even the West Coast. He had expected one of those to be the source, or at least that it was amphetamines. Most manufactured drugs could be traced to the source of the manufacturer by the contents of the capsules or pills. These orange tissues contained a completely unknown molecular structure. Jack couldn't rest until he had found the source.

He was still stretching when he heard what he thought was the lab door opening. It was to the front of him. Jack did not like working with his back to any door. So, he had positioned his working area in the direction of the main door. He was sure someone had entered the lab.

He glanced down at his watch.

Three-eleven a.m.

He frowned.

"Marilyn?" he called out, thinking perhaps his wife had, after all, become concerned and was making sure he was okay.

There was no answer, no further movement. Then he heard the soft "click" the door made as it shut. The lab door had an automatic self-closer. In an environment that required temperature control, an ordinary door would not have worked. It would have stayed open if left alone. Too many people never shut doors behind them, coming or going.

Jack knew every sound in his lab, every hum and click of every machine. He even knew the sound of the refrigerator walk-in as it went off and on during its cycle.

Every sound.

He *knew* the door had opened and closed.

He kept staring at the corner of a cabinet, the spot

where someone would have to appear as they came through the lab door and toward his workstation. After a few minutes, when no one appeared, he frowned then shrugged. He turned back to his microscope. If he was beginning to hear noises, he'd been here too long.

He was too tired, however, to accomplish anymore this night. His eyes burned. He started rubbing them. He would put his equipment and slides away and go home.

Suddenly, out of the corner of his eye, he caught a movement. It was to his right. It was in the shadows at the end of the room. He knew someone was there.

Jack's eyes were still blurry from having rubbed them too hard, but he knew what he saw. The person was dressed entirely in black. He'd always thought people at night dressed completely in black to minimize their exposure, to remain undetected.

But why would anyone want to come into the lab at this time of night and not let himself be known?

Something was wrong.

Jack rose slowly from the stool, still straining to see toward the door. His heart was racing. Who could it be?

Most people avoided the autopsy room and lab as if the dead might suddenly sit up and grab hold of them. It was a scary place to most. He had to admit that shelves of internal organs floating around acted as a natural deterrent to visitors. Most never came back a second time.

Again, he wondered who this could be.

He jerked his head to the left. He was sure he had seen someone move in front of the slide cabinet. Hadn't he?

He frowned again. This had gone beyond a prank. Every instinct and nerve in his body told him he was in danger. He felt the loudest sound in the room was that of his heart racing rapidly, his shallow breath coming in sharp gasps as his fear rose.

Yet, this was stupid. He willed his heart to slow down, to quit beating so rapidly. More than anyone, he knew these bodies were far beyond moving.

He went to his bed every night, went right to sleep, and slept soundly until his morning alarm woke him. He never had dreams or nightmares of bodies slowly rising, coming toward him, or becoming zombies. That happened only in the movies. Reality was quite different. Sometimes, he even enjoyed a good book by Dean Koontz or Stephen King in the evenings as a way to relax before going to bed.

No, there was nothing here to frighten him. At least, there was usually nothing here. He wasn't a person who scared easily. He had never been superstitious and prided himself on his rational thinking.

Jack felt the hair on his neck stand up.

A shiver rippled through him, causing him to break out in "goose bumps." He tasted his fear and had no rational explanation for it.

After all, this was his lab. He had worked here for many years, many months, many weeks, many days, many hours. He knew there was nothing here to hurt him. He had never been afraid before.

So why this inexplicable, absolute, helpless feeling that had suddenly and without warning engulfed him?

Within him, a voice shouted, *Run. Run for your life.*

But there was nowhere to run.

There was nowhere to hide.

The shadow moved toward him.

Chapter 22

Colton had to slow down a couple of blocks from the lab. Blue and red lights were everywhere.

Yes, he had turned his phone off last night to have a little personal time with Marsha, which he had not been able to do so much of since these homeless cases had started. He had been so exhausted he forgot to turn it back on when they finally went to sleep.

When he turned it back on this morning, there were dozens of missed calls, most of them from Pete.

He listened then went to Jack's lab immediately. He sensed the urgency in Pete's voice for him to get to Jack's lab.

What were all these police cars doing?

What was the ambulance doing there?

Colton stepped a few feet inside the lab, unable to believe what he was seeing. This just couldn't be true. Surely, he was still at home in bed, where he had been, sound asleep, in a deep sleep of total exhaustion, when the call had come to get to the lab ASAP.

He *had* to be asleep.

Back in his own bed.

The thought kept repeating in his mind.

And he was having his worst nightmare.

Jack was not only dead, his body had been brutally and completely torn apart.

Wait, a part of Colton's brain cried. *Maybe it isn't Jack, after all.* Jack had several assistants under him. Maybe it was one of them. Maybe it was even the janitor or the maintenance man, having come in for some equipment repair. Something. It had to be someone besides Jack.

Maybe it was—

Colton shook his head. He was in a sudden, complete act of denial here. He couldn't seem to shake it. Since the moment he had stepped through the tiny entrance to the lab and spotted the body, or the main part of it, on the floor, he had not moved.

His eyes were riveted to the mutilated figure. For some reason, he could not look away.

No! No! No!

Not Jack.

Not Jack, who was so full of life, so vibrant, so *alive*.

The numbness began wearing off to the sounds of retching coming from the lab's adjoining washroom and break area.

Whoever was in there, he would not be the only one.

Colton was finally able to bring himself to look around the room, focusing on the people there. There were several young officers here, rookies really, just new to the force. Now, who would send them to this? Of course, they would eventually have to deal with situations like this and probably the sooner, the better. One of them was probably the one in the washroom right now.

Colton looked at their faces, anywhere but at the body. Each face was a mask, fixed in various positions and postures, from disbelief to physical illness. One of the young men glanced toward the washroom, taking a step toward it. The one in there had better hurry or he would have company whether he wanted it or not.

If Colton had seen his own face, it would have matched the others. They all could have been actors in some bizarre play, caught in a frieze in the last tragic scene.

Although he had been on the force long enough to have moved up from "clean" murders to the more brutal ones, when one came so close to home like this, it was different.

And this was as different as it got.

Taking a deep breath, Colton looked around the room.

Better take a deep one now, he thought, *'cause in a little while, the air will become unbearable.*

Blood was everywhere. It was splattered against walls, counters, shelves, equipment. One glass-fronted cabinet, where slides and other glassware were kept, was completely covered. The amount of blood thrown against the glass had been so profuse and thick that large globs of it had run down the glass and dripped down on the table below, forming a dark pool on the tabletop. The blood had run under a centrifuge machine. Blood was smeared on the wooden frame of the cabinet, around the handle. The door was not completely closed.

Colton carefully took several steps to the cabinet. He glanced down. On the counter was a long, glass stir stick that somehow had been missed when the blood flew.

Colton reached into his pocket, bringing out plastic gloves and pulling them onto both hands. He picked up the stir stick and used it to open the left door of the cabinet.

Just as he thought, the contents of the cabinet were in disarray, with the appearance of having been rummaged through, as if someone had been looking for something.

He turned around to survey the rest of the cabinets, noting they all had been ransacked. He looked down again at Jack or what was left of him.

Jack, the brilliant one, who had gone through all that schooling, so he could get off the streets.

Jack, who wanted a clean, safe job so his family would be secure.

Jack, who had done all he could in his beloved profession so that his wife, Marilyn, would not have to worry about his coming home in one piece.

Jack, oh, Jack.

Colton felt a tear form in each eye and fall down his cheeks as he blinked. He was not ashamed to cry for this man, his friend, in front of the rest of these men.

Colton had cried at other crime scenes when the body had been obviously tortured, then mutilated, maybe before, maybe after death.

No one should have to die like this. It was—

"Colton?"

One of the men had approached him, effectively bringing his thoughts back to the matters at hand, causing him to forget his own thoughts. He jumped.

"Sorry, man," the assistant ME was saying, knowing that whatever he said would be totally inadequate. He knew the friendship that had existed between these two.

"Thanks," Colton responded automatically, his voice hoarse. He cleared his throat.

Nothing further was said for a few minutes. He watched a lab tech scrape a glob of Jack's brains off a doorframe. The man put it into a plastic bag, carefully drawing his fingers across the zip lock opening.

Usually, these men chatted with each other as they worked. There would be comments of "here's another," or "ah, look at this," as they found some small piece that might be used as evidence to help solve the crime. They were experts at their jobs and knew how important their task was.

But now they worked in complete silence, wondering if they would complete their work before they also got sick, one by one.

Colton squatted down beside Jack's body, sitting slightly forward, his hands hanging limply in front, arms resting on his knees.

One of Jack's arms was missing.

A large, plastic bag was shoved into his view. Inside was an arm, the shoulder joint was a jagged mass of flesh and bone.

Ripped off. The arm had obviously been ripped off.

Who was strong enough to do that?

Some punk on PCP or bad dope, bad *orange* dope?

Where had that thought come from?

Colton took the bag from whoever had handed it to him. He held it for a few seconds, then it seemed as if it were red hot. He quickly put it aside.

Jack's throat had been completely torn open as if gigantic claws had dug into one side of his throat and raked across, creating a deep, six-rutted gouge across his throat.

The jugular vein had done its usual job of pumping out blood when ripped open. Jack's head was covered in blood. His eyes were torn out in the same manner as the throat, downward across the face.

The lower jawbone had been totally ribbed away from the upper part of the skull. They had found it across the room, and it now rested in its own ziplocked plastic bag, just like the left arm.

Colton just hoped against hope that Jack had already been dead before most of this slaughter had taken place.

The rest of the body seemed intact, although one foot was turned completely opposite around on the ankle than how it was supposed to be. Who, again, had the strength to do that? Who had the strength to pull a skull apart like that?

Specimens.

Jack had become parts.

Specimens.

Evidence.

Jack-in-a-bag.

Colton almost lost control at that point and started to giggle at that thought. He knew he was on the verge of becoming hysterical. He didn't mean to have irreverent thoughts about his friend, but this situation brought them to mind.

How to deal with this?

Colton jerked his head up, looking up quickly. He heard another man in the washroom.

Pete? Was Pete here?

At that moment Pete walked up to Colton. Colton hadn't noticed him before. Perhaps it had been Pete in the washroom when Colton first came in.

Why not? Experience never had you prepared for something like this. No one blamed anyone for any reaction to this carnage.

"I can't even think where to begin," Pete said, his voice flat, devoid of expression.

Colton looked at his partner. Pete looked as if he had aged. The lines of his face appeared deeper.

"Robbery?" Pete ventured to ask. He almost felt foolish asking. What was in here? Bodies? Some specialized glassware? True, the equipment was quite expensive, but nothing appeared to be missing. That stuff couldn't be fenced very easily, anyway. Not any drugs usable to anyone, just those used by Jack during his work.

Colton was only half listening to Pete who didn't care if anyone was listening or not. He was talking to himself, trying to make some sense of this. "Obviously, he put up a good fight, by the looks of the place."

"Yeah, Jack would," Colton answered for the first time. He was still not completely listening, though.

Who knew what you knew, old friend? Colton's thoughts were racing. *Yeah, who knew you knew about the drug and who didn't want you telling it—*

What a thought, he realized. Why should this have anything to do with the drug and the overdose cases? Where had that idea come from?

Colton felt Pete's hand on his shoulder. He shook his head, coming out of his reverie.

He realized the techs were standing around, probably finished.

"Commander?" one of them asked.

"Yeah. Put the body and all the—the—evidence—" Colton choked on the words and had to take a deep breath before he could continue. "—and put them in a bag, in a drawer. The assistants can get to them as soon as they can."

It would be a rough autopsy for someone.

"You ready for the cleanup crew?" he asked.

They nodded agreement.

"I want to check a few more things here, then I'll call them."

The apparent motive did, indeed, appear to be robbery. The drawers and the cabinets had been ransacked, their contents thrown all over the room.

But what was here anyone would kill for, if not evidence of something?

Colton told Pete he would go tell Marilyn, Jack's wife. He knew her so well. How could he tell her about this? But he knew he had to.

The instant she opened the door and saw his face and another officer behind him, she fainted.

Colton caught her as she fell. He carried her to the sofa.

Chapter 23

The man was afraid he had given himself away when he had laughed, but it had been a spontaneous outcry of pure joy, pure power.

Sensing the sorrow Colton felt in losing his best friend, especially in the way he had "died," made the man laugh.

For a second, when he felt perhaps Colton had heard him, he thought he was exposed.

Then the knowledge he held of these puny humans, how they let things like grief and other emotions engulf them, override their ability to think clearly let him know he had felt Colton before Colton felt him.

Had Colton perceived this man's laugh for even a few more seconds he would have touched him, and he would have known exactly what had happened to Jack, who had done it and why.

But Colton had let his grief overcome his other senses and that was just fine with this man.

The man knew exactly how to defeat Colton and Abby, what would kill them.

Patience.

Soon—*soon.*

Chapter 24

T he funeral was particularly hard on Denver, as a city having lost one of its highly skilled police-men, but it was especially hard on Colton.

Marilyn's mother and sister had come to be with her, but she asked that Colton help her with the arrangements of the funeral.

It fell to the department to arrange it, of course. Not only police and military representatives from Denver and Colorado attended, but persons from across the country came to pay their respects to one of their fallen.

They would have come because of his position, but the way he was killed evoked additional responses from all over the country.

Bagpipers from all the clubs around Denver played "Amazing Grace," which had become the traditional song to be played at these types of funerals.

It was all Colton could do to keep from crying for his friend as he helped carry the casket to the front of the church. He knew the background of this song. A sea chief of police named John Newton was part of the Atlantic slave trade in the early-to-middle-1750s. During a partic-ularly terrible storm at sea, he asked God for mercy and started writing the words to his song, depicting the "amazing grace" that he received from God. He finally quit the slave trade, became a minister, and finished the song. It was now the most popular and most widely used song at funerals and evangelical church services that had ever been written.

Colton sat next to Marilyn during the graveside service. He knew that many criminals returned to the scene of the crime just to witness what he or she had done. That was part of the thrill of what had happened, whether that was murder, arson, rape or whatever.

He refused to look around and perhaps give this…whatever it was…the pleasure of Colton wondering about him.

Colton would not have known the person he wanted if he saw him. The killer had taken the form of a middle-aged man with sandy hair, a neatly-trimmed short beard, and mustache. His business suit screamed success. He also took great care to not emit any feelings or emotions.

He gloated in this victory, or so he thought, over Colton.

Marilyn laid Jack to rest at her small, family cemetery beside her church. She placed a bench at the foot of his grave. She, and others, could see the beautiful Rocky Mountains as they sat, meditated, and thought of Jack.

❧❦❧

Colton had taken the day after Jack's murder off, to help Marilyn and compose himself, but now he plopped himself down in one of the swivel chairs in front of a computer and gave himself a shove away from the desk. He rolled easily over next to a middle-aged lady whose fingers were flying across the keyboard.

"Hi, Colton," she said, smiling, although she did not

look away from the monitor until she had entered the last of her commands. Then she swirled around to smile at him.

"Long time, no see," she said.

Colton smiled in return. "You are amazing on that thing," he commented, referring to her ability with the computer.

Jennie just shrugged. "If it's the only thing you do eight hours a day, you must get good. I'm just glad not to be using a typewriter," she replied. "You have to want something. I know you're not so captivated by my charms and great beauty that you'd give up any of your precious detecting time to visit me," she teased him.

"How about your brains, then?" he asked.

"Now, that's a different story. What can I help you with?"

Whatever she was in the middle of, she would stop for Colton. Most of them in the computer lab would. He was just that kind of guy. Several of the ladies in the room had been heard to say out loud they wished he weren't so happily married, or even married at all.

"A big order, I'm afraid. But I'm perfectly sure you can handle it."

She smiled again. "Flattery will get you everywhere, you know."

Colton laughed. He liked this lady. They were very comfortable with each other. She didn't try any female charms on him, and they knew where they stood with each other.

"As I said, a tall order," he began. "I need all telephone calls that went from Denver to Midland, Arkansas, and vice versa, those from Midland to Denver, within, say, the last three months."

"Don't you mean Midland, Texas?" she asked. She had never heard of Midland, Arkansas.

"No. Arkansas. It's a small town just south of Fort Smith. I'm talking really small town here, so there can't be many calls."

Her eyebrows went up. She had been picturing many, many pages of calls.

"It can't be many. Honest. Midland has about five hundred people in it. How many of those do you think call Denver for anything?"

"Ordering Bronco tickets?" Jennie ventured.

He just looked at her.

"You're kidding, of course," she said.

"Nope. I need to know. Think you can handle it?"

"Well, I don't know," she said. She was smiling again. "Might take a while."

Colton stood up, whirling the chair back to its place. He turned back to her.

"Do your best, okay?"

"Always. Interesting case?"

"You've read about the serial killer that seems to be killing in a spiral around the Metro area?"

"Yeah, who hasn't? The 'Spiral Murders' the papers are calling it. It's got southeast part of Denver wondering who will be killed there. Have you driven by Bible Park in the evening lately? Hardly anyone walks or jogs, or even walk their dogs. No one wants to end up in the Canal, you know."

"You're not being foolish yourself and still jogging there, are you? Trying to act like a tough lady cop and it can't happen to you?"

His tone was light, but Jennie knew he was concerned about her.

When she didn't answer, he knew he had hit on the truth.

"Well?" He was going to make her admit it.

"Okay, I'll stop. But it's been okay so far."

He just continued to look at her.

"So, okay. I promise, all right? I'll quit jogging at Bible Park."

"Or any park right now."

"Rosamond?" she tried again.

"No. Who knows? Although southeast Denver seems to be the next target area of the spiral, the killer may decide to change his route. You know anything can happen with a psycho like that."

"I know. You have my word. No jogging." She gestured toward the computer. "What does a small town in Arkansas have to do with this case?"

She was a sworn police officer, not just a civilian computer tech. She would not say anything to anyone about a case.

"I'm not sure," he admitted. "It may just be a wild hair idea of mine. But I have a theory I want to check out, and I need to know about any calls. And I need it on the QT, okay? Remember, this is just my own theory right now."

"Aw, the plot thickens. That's what I love about this job." She shrugged. "You'll have it ASAP."

"Thanks. I owe you."

"Just have Marsha make one of her delicious Mississippi Mud pies for me and we'll call it even."

Colton laughed. "You got it," he said, putting his thump up.

"And, Colton," she said, softly. "Thanks for being concerned about me. About the jogging, I mean."

"Hey, we couldn't lose our best computer programmer, now could we?" He smiled. He started to turn away then remembered something. "Oh, yeah, but sure to include calls to and from pay phones with that list, okay?"

Her eyebrows shot up again, but, before he reached the door, she had turned back to the computer.

The report would be a piece of cake.

Chapter 25

Not again.

Colton groaned when the phone rang. It was not far from his ear. He was always instantly awake whenever it broke a peaceful, deep sleep with its harsh, raucous tone. But they did not turn the bell down for fear he would be so deeply asleep he would not awaken.

Marsha simply moaned and rolled over to her other side. She pulled the blanket with her as she went. This left Colton exposed to the cool Denver night air clad only in his undershorts.

They were not using the central heat yet. During mid-to-late September the days were beautiful and warm in Denver. Temperatures could be from sixty-five to seventy-five degrees during the day. Accompanied by a cool mountain breeze, these days seemed ideal to Colton.

But the nights could get quite chilly during this time of the year. Tonight was no exception. He supposed they should start using the heat, but it would make the house too warm during the day.

He started shivering right away, but he didn't bother to fight Marsha for any of the blanket. A phone call now could only mean that he would be getting dressed and going to some crime scene. He glanced at the clock with the large digital numbers as he quickly reached for the phone.

Six a.m. Already?

It wasn't even light yet, but that was also common for this time of year. There could also be clouds out on the eastern plains. That would keep it darker longer.

Well, at least it was an almost decent time to be getting up. He usually was up at six-thirty, anyway.

He lifted the receiver just as he felt it starting to ring again. There was a soft "ping" as it came off the base.

"Yeah?" he asked softly. No use waking Marsha. She would know where he was if he was gone when she got up. That routine had long been established between them. She never worried. He would call as soon as he could.

"We've got another one."

Pete's voice sounded tired. Maybe it was still just sleepy.

"Where are you?" Colton asked.

"I'm still at home but ready to leave. They called me first because I'm closest to this one."

"Where?" asked Colton. He felt he could probably guess at least the general area. Southeast Denver.

He was right.

"Rosamond Park," Pete responded. "You know, down on Tamarac before you get to I-Two-Twenty-Five. Beautiful place. Well, usually," he added quickly.

Colton knew what he meant.

"Male? Female?" Colton asked.

"Female. Around forty to fifty, somewhere along there, at first glance, they said. She's got sweats and running shoes on. Probably having an early morning walk or run. That's all I know 'til we get there."

"I'm on my way," Colton replied as he hung up.

It only took him a few minutes to get dressed. *Do it enough times, and it becomes second nature.* He tiptoed silently out of the bedroom, gently closing the door. Marsha could be a real bear if she didn't get enough sleep.

"Rosamond Park?" he asked himself. "Now, where have I heard that recently? Rosamond Park…hmm…"

His hand was on the doorknob when he remembered where he had heard it. Jennie. Hadn't she teased him about jogging in Rosamond Park if she couldn't go to Bible?

It couldn't be.

Maybe she had not taken him seriously.

When did Jennie jog? Mornings? Evenings? He realized he didn't know. They were friends, but some things had just never come up as a topic of conversation. And they had only touched on it the other day.

He couldn't leave without calling her. He didn't care if he did wake her up. He had to know that she was safe.

He dialed her number clumsily, almost missing the correct buttons on the number pad a couple of times.

In the middle of the third ring, the receiver on the other end was lifted. It dropped with a loud "thud" on a table. Colton held his receiver away from his ear. He heard a faint "shit" from someone in the background but he couldn't tell if it was her voice or not.

"This better be good," her voice said. It was a sleepy voice. It was a very unhappy voice at having been awakened, but, nevertheless, it *was* her voice.

"Jennie! Thank God. You're okay," he breathed into the phone.

"Colton? Is that you? Of course, I'm okay, aside from the fact that you just woke me up on my day off. You've never called me at home before so why shouldn't I be okay?"

"Sorry, I just had to make sure. I just got a call from

Pete. A woman about your age has been found murdered at Rosamond Park. You mentioned jogging at Rosamond. I didn't know if you might decide it really couldn't happen to you and go there."

"Hey, I promised, didn't I?" she asked. Then he heard her catch her breath. "You know what, though? I almost did go there last evening, right before dark. Even though I promised, I almost did. You know, that could have been me, do you realize that? Only my promise to you made me stay home, have a swim in the indoor pool instead. Oh, God."

He knew the realization that it *could* have been her hit her hard.

"Thanks, Colton, for making me promise. And thanks for caring."

"No problem. Talk to you later," he said.

He hung up and headed out the door.

Colton was in a foul mood by the time he arrived at the office. This was Thursday. He had asked Jennie for that phone list early Monday morning. The week had gone quickly. It seemed the days flew by with the whole force holding its breath, waiting for the next murder to be reported.

Extra patrols and routes had been scheduled, trying to keep a continual police presence in Southeast Denver.

They were getting calls all day and all night long. It seemed every time someone heard a noise outside or in the alley, they called the police to come.

When the next murder did take place, in Rosamond Park, they had no more clues now than they did when the first murder took place. The official clues had disappeared with Jack's murder.

Only Jack's few casually spoken words to Colton the day before he was killed that night had started the wheels turning in Jack's mind.

Colton felt ragged, used up by the time he turned his car into the driveway of his home.

Talk about sensory and emotional overload. He had sure been bombarded with too much today. He had not had time to sit and absorb any of the incidents.

Then, to realize that all the events—Abby's actions, the killings, the orange candy—might be related was certainly too much.

He had talked to several of the downtown business owners today about the homeless who had been murdered.

One of the victims helped others as much as he could. One man said that several times when he had hangovers, this man had helped him. One homeless man he talked to, who was now a reporter for a local newspaper, said the same man had saved his life when he first came to Denver to live on the streets. He had come from Arkansas and was not used to the cold in Denver. He had found himself some old carpeting and a large cardboard box. The victim had come over to him, kicked the box, and told him to come with him. He had a lean-to, a shelter, and let the man stay with him. The reporter had about six inches of snow on him when he was found. He felt sure he would have frozen to death if the victim had not realized someone was in the carton and took him with him.

Staff members at St. Francis Hospital cried when they found out one of the victims was this same man. They recalled how several months back he had delivered a stirring eulogy for one of the other homeless who had died. He also asked the staff about their families and how everyone was doing. They said he would come in, get showered and shaved and cleaned up, and would look like he was worth a million dollars.

When it came to helping out at one of the local shelters, this same man volunteered to clean the bathrooms and handle other jobs that no one else wanted to do. One nurse had just seen him a few days before he was killed but had been gone for a few months and did not know he had been killed.

When he "cleaned up," he would say that he was going to straighten his life up and he seemed to mean it. She would always think, *This time, he's really going to do it.*

He was an alcoholic but a lot of fun to be with when he was sober, and he was willing and able to learn just about anything. He was fluent in both English and Spanish. One problem, though, was that he alternately told staff that he was from California, Chicago, and Texas. The coroner had been unable to find any family for him.

This man had been found not far from one of the other victims. The other man was also familiar to the staff. They remembered that he was so smart he could do any trig problem he was given.

He was found in the tract of undeveloped land in the Central Platte Valley.

This particular homeless man often worked day jobs out of a local temporary work service.

Police had questioned several young transients about the deaths but released them. They had no other clues.

Colton knew he wouldn't sleep tonight. Marsha would. Somehow, she had acquired the ability to listen to his problems, sympathize, help him talk through them, yet disassociate herself. She could let go and rest. As soon as her head hit the pillow, she was out.

Of course, she had her own career during the day, one that kept her busy, so she was tired when it came time to go to bed.

He smiled when he thought about her. For the past six years now that they had been married, she had been a wonderful wife.

Several of his friends had experienced divorces. Their wives just had not been able to handle the demands that being a police officer put on their husbands, them, and the family. But Marsha had been a brick.

He made a special effort to be with her and Abby. When he found out six years ago that he had a daughter and then rescued her from death, he wasn't about to lose either of them.

Marsha had been his high school sweetheart and evidently had been pregnant when they parted. He went off to college and she went apparently to visit an aunt in California. She never told him she was pregnant.

Colton forgave her whatever personal reasons she had for not telling him. And the circumstances surrounding their reunion were so incredible and unbelievable he did not bother to tell anyone. If the subject came up he just laughed and said, "It must have been 'The Force' that did it."

That was closer to the truth than he wanted to admit, but he wouldn't try to explain it. No one would believe it and just start thinking he was crazy.

But now he needed to talk to Abby.

Chapter 26

Colton reached for the phone. He was going to call Jennie. He didn't want to pressure her, but this was the longest she had ever taken with a report.

"Jennie?"

"Hi, Colton. What's happening? Did the phone numbers help you?"

"What phone numbers? I've never received a report from you. That's what I was calling about. You've never taken this long before."

"I don't understand," responded Jennie. Her voice sounded puzzled. Colton could almost see the frown on her expressive face. "I sent the report up to you the next morning," she said. "I gave it to Vicki myself. When she got back, she said she had put it right on your desk, on top of everything, so you couldn't miss it."

Vicki was their in-house courier. She was working on her degree in law enforcement at the University of Denver, and her work-study program put her here.

"Damn. It's not here now. I've been wondering about you. It wasn't your usual efficient method of doing things."

"Honest. I sent it up to you."

"Oh, I believe you. It's just missing, that's all. How about running another one?"

"Sure. I've got a long program running right now that'll take a while, but then I'll get right on it."

"Thanks, Jennie."

She had not indicated, in any way, that she minded doing the program again, but he felt bad having to ask her. He had no doubt she'd done it.

Just then one of the young rookies walked up to him. The rookie was holding up a piece of paper that he was starting to read from.

"Colton, listen to this. I have a few ideas—"

Colton couldn't believe it. The man was holding a piece of paper with telephone numbers on the side toward Colton. "Give me that," he said. At the same time, he reached out and yanked the piece of paper out of the man's hands, crumbling part of it.

"Hey. What's the deal?" the rookie asked.

"Where did you get this? Off my desk, by any chance?"

"No, of course not. I don't touch anything on your desk."

The young man had taken a step backward, cringing at the fury in Colton's voice.

"Then where? Answer me."

"The—the floor—a couple of days ago, I guess. It was on the floor, there by your wastebasket."

"You always use paper from the trash?" Colton asked. He was still very angry and had raised his voice without realizing it.

The other people in the room had stopped what they were doing to stare at the two of them and listen. They wondered what the young man had done to warrant such an outburst from Colton.

"I—I was walking by your desk when I had a sudden

idea about the case. I reached down and took the paper to my desk, writing my thoughts on the back. You know how I am about paper on the floor. And I saw I could use the backside of it, not waste it."

He was right, Colton knew. The young man was always straightening things. His desk was the neatest in the room.

"I've been waiting on this telephone report all week, that's all. That important, yes."

Colton slowly turned to his left, where another man was hoping not to be noticed. A fan on his desk was oscillating, causing papers to ripple on several desks, including Colton's.

Colton had complained about the fan before, how it scattered everything.

At Colton's look, the man reached over and turned the fan off. As the fan died, the men in the room remained silent.

"If I see another sheet of paper on my desk moved, even a fraction of an inch, that fan's going where the sun don't shine."

He whirled around and sat down at his desk, straightening out the page and starting to run his finger down the list.

Slowly the figures in the room started to move, as if in slow motion, moving out of a tableau to another scene.

The young man started to turn away. His face was very expressive, although he was trying to hide the hurt he was feeling.

"Jon," Colton called softly.

Jon heard him and turned back.

"Sorry, man," Colton began, running his hand through his hair. "I was out of line, yelling at you like that. You had no idea it was anything anybody needed."

The young man relaxed. Colton saw the tension go out of his body.

"We're all more than a little uptight, sir," he said. This was his way of forgiving Colton.

"Ain't it the truth?"

"Sir," the young man said. He nodded and turned away. He felt good about himself now.

They all would forgive Colton. This wasn't the Colton they knew and loved, but they did understand. There still were no clues as to who the killer was. Then there was the murder of Jack, Colton's best friend. They were all beginning to feel the tension.

Colton saw what he knew would be there. Several calls had been placed to Denver from Midland. The calls had been from payphones to payphones, however, so there was no way to trace the parties involved.

It proved part of this theory—his personal theory. Somehow these murders were connected to the incident six years ago, and they were connected to him.

But there was still nothing tangible he could prove. No proof or evidence he could take to the chief and be right.

This was completely up to Colton.

Colton thought he remembered Jack saying that the only one he had told about his findings, so far, was Colton. Evidently not, though, or someone else would not have known to take the notebook containing the clues.

On the heels of that thought, however, was the question of why. Why would anyone take them? The only one interested in them would be the killer, right? Well, Colton himself, of course, in hopes of using them to track and capture the killer, but aside from him, who else but the killer? And if the killer, then how did he even know about them?

Colton leaned back and shut his eyes, interlocking

his fingers behind his head. He put his feet on his desk, one ankle crossed over the other. He tried to think back at the time he and Jack had talked about the strange drug. Where had they been when they were talking about it?

The most obvious times were in the lab, the cafeteria of the hospital, and the parking lot of the hospital. Many people had come and gone back and forth past them at the hospital. Had anyone stopped to listen or been close enough to hear what they were saying?

Colton brought the scene in the parking lot back to mind—the cars, the trees, people walking by. Yes, there had been one man. He was a couple of cars away, and he had his trunk up, as if he were looking for something in it. Yes, the man had been there the whole time. He could have seen Jack put his briefcase up on Colton's car, open it, and take out the little notebook Jack carried every-where. He could have seen Jack open it up, start to show Colton something, then close it.

Were they talking loud enough for the man to hear?

They could have been—if the man had a directional mic in his trunk, pointing their way.

Stop it, Colton, he told himself. *Electronic surveil-lance, is it now?* He smiled at himself, guessing even cops watched too much TV. As far as he knew, no one in the parking lot even knew who they were. They had both been wearing Dockers and sports shirts, comfortable shoes. Jack had even worn sandals that day. There was nothing about either of them that said "cop."

Colton sat up quickly, his palms slapping the desk. He was tired of having his imagination run away with him like this.

This was the real world, not some spy show with vans full of electronic gadgets or shoes with heels full of bullets. No one had a microphone disguised as a pen or a mirror on his sunglasses.

Shades of Agent 86!

The world was not like Inspector Gadget. Save those things for the movies.

Colton had only glanced at the page Jack had opened his notebook to. He was trying to remember what he had seen or read there. He had seen something on that page that could be important, but it eluded him. It simply would not come to mind.

He slapped his palms down on the desk again, causing several heads to turn his way. Then he slapped his forehead. The others just shook their heads and turned back to their own reports. They knew what was happening. All of them had, at one time or another, forgotten something, failed to write something down, then couldn't recall it when it looked to be important. They knew the frustration and anger that came from not remembering something they knew they should.

Colton shook his head. What he had glanced at and his brain had recorded was right on the tip of his tongue, but he just couldn't remember.

It was just one of those things that would probably cause him to jerk awake in the middle of the night with total recall. Then, it would take forever to get back to sleep, if sleep would come at all.

Jack was always making his own notes, sometimes just thoughts that brought other thoughts that had nothing to do with the case he was working on. Colton had once seen "milk" on a page in Jack's notebook when it was open on the counter in the lab.

"Milk," he had asked. "Did you find traces of milk in his stomach?"

Colton was referring to the case they were working on.

"Huh?" Jack had responded, looking up from where he was poking around in some organ in the body.

"What?"

"Milk," Colton had repeated. "You have 'milk' as the last entry here. Was that the last thing he had before death?"

"Oh, oh, no," Jack had replied, absent-mindedly. "Marilyn called earlier and asked me to bring some on the way home."

"Oh," Colton had said, flatly. He was strangely dis-appointed.

Maybe this was one of those times. Whatever Colton had seen, it probably wasn't important at all. Probably the only thing he had time to glance at before Jack closed the thing was one of those silly entries of Jack's, totally unrelated to this case.

But what if it were important? Colton couldn't shake the feeling that if he could remember what he saw, he could figure out why someone wanted the notebook, and by knowing why, he would know who.

Oh, yeah, Super-Cop, aren't you? He said to himself. *Give me a red cape and everything will fall into place.*

Chapter 27

Colton slowly and carefully removed the covers and just as quietly swung his legs over the side of the bed. He did not want to wake up Marsha.

He knew it would come like this. He knew he would remember the letters, or the word, whichever it would turn out to be, while he was asleep, right in the middle of making love to Marsha, or sometime during some other important occasion. That was the nature of the beast. The brain seemed to remember things it had seen at the most inopportune times. Sometimes it was just trivial things it recalled.

In this case, Colton hoped it was important.

It had come while he was sleeping. He knew enough to get up right away and write it down or he was liable to forget it.

Even famous authors said that when they woke up with plots and conversations, they immediately got up and wrote them down or they were likely to forget and never remember the same thing the same way again.

He slipped on house shoes and quietly padded out of the bedroom. The study was the best place to turn on extra lights and not wake anyone else up.

He sat down, pulling a telephone pad toward him while reaching for a pen at the same time.

He wrote:

ADB

That's what he had seen on the page Jack had started to show him from his notebook.

For some reason, Jack had changed his mind about talking to Colton right then and had shut his notebook.

Colton was sure, though, that he had seen ADB.

No.

He shook his head. Those were the three letters he had seen, but, actually, Jack had written them differently. They had been more like ABD.

Maybe they had even been Abd.

Yeah, that was it. Abd.

But did they have a period after them, or not? Did it even matter? Colton wasn't clear on that point.

Abd.

Colton looked again at what he had written. He shook his head. The three letters made no sense at all. What did they mean?

Knowing Jack, maybe it had been apples, bread, and dog food for Marilyn, to be picked up at the store on the way home.

No, Jack had been on to something about the drug that had killed all these people. Colton was sure of that. And Jack had been so sure of whatever it was that he had stayed most of the night investigating it. He had been so sure of something that he had given his life for it.

Hell, someone else was so sure that Jack was so sure that he—or she—had *taken* Jack's life to erase whatever it was. *Taken* was not the word—brutalized, slaughtered was more like it. At least the autopsy had revealed that Jack died quickly, with all the carnage coming post-death.

That, at least, had brought some peace of mind to Colton and Jack's family.

Colton leaned back in his chair, tossing the pen onto the desk as he did so. He was wide-awake now.

What exactly had Jack said in the parking lot? Something about the victims being drugged.

Colton frowned. On top of the orange tint to the skin after death, which dissipated after a while, what else had Jack seen?

Yes, the people had OD'd. That much was certain. That was what went down on the death certificates of each of these victims. But why would Jack say "drugged" instead of the more common expression of "OD'd?" Most people didn't refer to drug overdoses as the person being "drugged." That term was usually meant for a person who had been slipped a Mickey Finn, sodium pentothal, the date-rape drug, or something like that.

"No, that's not what Jack said," Colton recalled, thinking out loud in the silent room. It was something like "drugged," but not quite that.

Drug toxicity.

That was it.

That's what Jack had said.

Are you sure? a nagging voice from within asked him. *Which one was it? Drugged or drug toxicity?*

Drug toxicity.

He was sure.

Now, the question was what did Jack mean by that? Colton needed a good medical dictionary for that. To be more specific, he needed the book that published all known drugs, characteristics of those drugs, side effects, the whole ball of wax. He didn't personally own one, but he knew someone who did. And he would be seeing that someone tomorrow.

Oh, Jack, Jack, he cried. *Why were you so damned*

intelligent? And who did you talk to? You told someone what you knew, besides me.

But who?

Colton knew if he could just find out who Jack had talked to those last few days, even hours maybe, that he would be near the murderer.

Who?

Chapter 28

Colton was doodling on his pad at his desk the next day when one of the men stopped.

The letters had stayed on his mind.

"Doing your ABCs there, Colton?" The man smiled, teasing. "I know we're back to square one, but this is ridiculous."

"Oh, hi," Colton said, acknowledging the man. He leaned back, tossing his pencil on top of the paper. He had printed and written Abd all over a piece of paper.

Abd
Abd
Abd
Abd
Abd
Abd
Abd

"Just remembering something Jack had written down," Colton continued. "I have no idea what it means, but it won't go away. It's really bugging me."

One of the other men paused as he passed by. The

mention of Jack's name caught his attention. He leaned over at looked at the page. "Knowing Jack, it could have been anything," he said.

"Yeah, I know, and that's part of the problem," Colton agreed. "Yet somehow it seems important."

They didn't question his feelings. He had established a reputation for being right about things, for just "feeling" things.

The first man was interested. "How were these letters written? Their order?" he asked.

Colton was quick to catch on. "You think that's important?" he asked him.

"Could be. You never know. Can you remember? Upper case? Lower case? Some upper, some lower? How?"

Colton sighed, letting out his breath. "That's been one of the things that have worried me. I'm just not sure. I saw them for only a split second. Why?"

The man shrugged. "Well, my kid's been studying the craziest thing in Biology class. At least, to me, it's crazy. I just don't see the need for a kid to have to memorize the scientific names of plants and animals. Maybe the technical name, yes, but not that long Latin name they give to everything. They find a new fossil and give it a name."

"Hey, did you read about the discovery of a third life form?" another man asked. "It's a microbe, but you can bet they stuck a name on it. My kid was counting something in the paper the other night. I asked him what he was doing, and he said he was seeing how many letters were in the name of the new life form. Seems there were thirteen in the first name and ten in the last name."

The first man turned back to Colton. "That's why I asked about the letters. Jack was always diagnosing microbes and bacteria and things like that. He wrote those things down, didn't he? Did you get this out of the lab report?"

"It's missing."

"Uh-oh," the man said. "Think he found something about something?"

Colton shrugged. He wasn't about to let anyone know what he knew at this point. "About these letters. What are you getting at?"

"Well, I'd check the scientific name of bacteria, if I were you. Maybe he found out what killed one of the bodies there in the morgue, and someone didn't like it. Obviously, he was killed for some reason."

Colton just looked at him. "You're right. Seems that nowadays psychos don't have to have a reason. But Jack shouldn't have to die for nothing."

Several of the men had stopped their work to listen to this conversation.

"Makes sense to me," one of them said. "We can't ignore anything that might be even the slightest clue in these cases."

"What?" Colton asked.

"To check out those letters as possible abbreviations for bacteria or microbes or some other kind of organism. Jack wrote them down for some reason. Right?"

"Right. I hadn't thought that far yet, but you guys could be on to something. So, who wants to gather up some journals and medical dictionaries for me? Let's check out the names of all known drugs while we're at it. Maybe it's the name of a drug."

"Jon, what about you? You have time for this?"

"Sure, it's part of the investigation, right?"

"Right," Colton agreed. It was a long shot, but he was willing for the men to keep busy, trying anything. They had no clues yet to Jack's killer. "Hey, where did you steal those?" he asked as he looked up to see one of the young officers, Ben, coming slowly between the desks. They young man was having quite a time keeping the whole stack in order.

"The library?" he answered, grinning.

"You know where that is, really?" another man asked.

"Ha, ha," Ben said.

"I thought you couldn't check out reference books," another added.

"You can't," was the reply.

"Well?" Colton asked.

"Now, Commander," Ben began. "You know a good cop never reveals his sources. After all, we don't know when we might have to check up on weird names again, now do we?"

"You're right. You're right. Ask me no questions—" Colton threw up his hands.

"—and I'll tell you no lies," Ben finished. He plopped them down on a long table in the conference room. "Come see what I've got.

Several men from the team gathered around the table, pulling books toward them.

"Whew," one said. "If we don't find it in one of these, it can't be found."

"Who's available?" Colton asked, looking up at the men.

"Several of us can get this done pretty quick, and Ben can get these back to wherever they came from."

Ben looked up and grinned. "I planned on doing that tonight, Commander, just a little before closing time."

He winked, and several men laughed. Ben's current girlfriend worked at the main branch of the Denver Library. They all knew it. The building wasn't far away.

"Yeah, play your cards right and this may be the big night."

"Could be, but only if I get these back this evening before they're missed."

Three men pulled up chairs and sat down around the table. Colton plopped down several pencils and pads of scratch paper just in case they found anything.

"What was that again, Commander? Capital ADB?"

"No, first letter upper case, next two lower case. Abd."

He wrote it in large letters on one of the pads and pushed it to the middle of the table where they all could see it.

"Could be the first letters of one word or the first letters of three words, or the first three of a second word, or"

"Okay, okay, we get the picture."

Several of the men groaned. But it was a good-natured group that started the word search.

It was a long shot, but anything was worth a try at this point. There were no other clues to the deaths that now had publicly been labeled as murders.

It seemed that Jack had left the only clue, if it could even be called one. Three letters written on a sheet of paper might not even have anything to do with these cases. Jack was notorious for scribbling all sorts of things down—things that only he knew the meaning of.

The only sounds for the next few minutes were the rustling and turning of pages. Colton looked at the bent heads studiously pouring over the books. No matter what a few special interest groups may say about police brutality, apathy, or lack of concern, he knew these men gave their jobs their very best. Especially these three here now. Whatever it had been, they probably would have volunteered to help do it. They really wanted to solve this case. These deaths were hanging over the whole department. As soon as they found out what they were looking for, perhaps they could come up with a plan of action to catch the guy.

"Commander, can we test these bodies again?"

"No can do. Jack said the condition dissipated after a time, after more decomposition. We wouldn't be able to prove a thing, at this point in time."

"Besides, three of the bodies have been claimed," one of the men added.

"Yeah," another agreed, looking up. "I just happened to be down there when the parents of one of them came in. Saddest thing. She told Davis they hadn't seen their son in five years. He'd run away from home after one particularly bad argument. Watching her nearly tore me apart. But her last words, 'at least now we know he's at peace,' really hit home." He shook his head. "Yeah, at least those loved ones can experience some closure. Not knowing where your relative was or what was happening would be worse than having a body to bury."

"That's right," one older man agreed. "A preacher once told me that when there was no body or even if the funeral had to be a closed casket, that the family reacted and took it in a completely different way than when you could see your loved one. They don't really want to believe their loved one is gone unless they see the body."

"I know what you mean," still another added. "I had a cousin killed in Vietnam. He was the driver of the lead truck of a convoy carrying ammunition when Charlie hit them. His truck was blown to smithereens. They sent back a sealed casket to my aunt that was supposed to be his body, but we all knew there was nothing in there since he was blown to bits. But my aunt never believed he was in that casket. Until the day she passed away years later, she swore he was a POW somewhere and that any day he would walk through the front door. She turned the whole house into a shrine for him."

They all shook their heads. They all had seen enough to understand.

A man stuck his head around the door. "What's up?" he asked.

"Just trying to check those letters we talked about earlier. Hoping they spell something."

"Oh, yeah," the man responded. "I got the article from my son about that third life form. Look."

He handed the newspaper article to Colton. Sure enough, scientists had proven the existence of a third life form.

One form of life was a bacterium, another was all animals and plants. This third, new one was called *Methanococcus jannaschii*, which Colton attempted to read out loud. Farther in the article it was referred to as *M. jannaschii*.

"See, that's what I meant earlier," the man said as he pointed to the abbreviated name. "They always abbreviate these things. That's why I asked you about the order and if there were dots, periods, between the letters or what. Maybe Jack himself had discovered another unknown life form, one that this murderer is putting into the bodies to kill them."

They were all looking at him in a funny way.

He shrugged. "Hey, anything is possible. Well, it's just an idea. But, hell, it's as good an idea as any, isn't it? We certainly don't have too more. I don't hear any of you guys coming up with anything."

He turned and walked out. He wasn't offended. He just had other work to do.

"He's right. We have *nada*."

"Doesn't seem to be anything here with those initials," one ventured. They looked at Colton. He had to agree as they all agreed by stopping. They pushed their chairs back, stretching as they stood up. Ben could take the books back tonight. They had not found anything, but they had to do it.

"Sure," he said. "Nothing here. Probably a stupid idea in the first place."

"No," Pete said. "We have to try everything, and this was worth a shot."

But it had given Colton an idea. It was a crazy idea, but why not? Weren't the rest of his feelings about these murders crazy? *Orange* poison? A spiral closing in on him? The killer part of a case six years ago? Why not add another crazy idea?

No one would ever know but him. If nothing came of it then no harm done.

If everything fell into place eventually, then he would be vindicated.

He was glad he had not given all the capsules to Jack. He was also glad Jack had given him one of the small vials. Just for safekeeping, Jack had said, as he laughed. How right he had been.

Colton went down the hall to the supply closet. He took a small FedEx Express mailing box, put the vial and capsule in it, along with a cover letter. He addressed it to a place he knew. He sealed the package himself and walked it downstairs, out the front door and deposited it in the FedEx pick-up box himself.

Why not? They had all just agreed they had to try everything and anything.

Chapter 29

As the elevator ascended to the tenth floor of the Cherry Tower here in Glendale, Colton thought about the lady he was coming to see.

Colton had asked Dr. Sally Knauer if he could meet her in her private office instead of her office at the police department.

He smiled to himself.

She had not sounded surprised at the request, and they had agreed on the time. Sure, he was right in the middle of the "serial killer" investigation. Some might think he was taking personal time when he should be working. The thing was, this was business. He just couldn't tell anyone else what he hadn't been able to completely tell himself.

Nothing made sense. Not the killings. Not the spiral pattern. Not Jack's seemingly senseless death.

Nothing.

He wanted the opinion of a professional psychiatrist, so he called Sally.

Also, deep down, he needed someone to talk to about Jack's death. Talking to Marsha always helped, but so did talking with Dr. Sally.

That's why she didn't sound surprised, he thought. *She thinks I'm going to talk about Jack. Hell, I probably will.*

The ping of the elevator stopping brought him out of his reverie.

As he turned right out of the elevator, he paused. Through the glass of the office in front of him—Dr. Sally's outer office and conference room—he had a breathtaking view of the Rocky Mountains.

Being ten floors up sure made a difference compared to his office on the sixth floor of the police building with a view of high rise office buildings outside his window.

A haze today dulled the view of the Rockies over the mountains, especially toward Mt. Evans. It was hard to see where the mountains ended and the sky began.

God, he loved this place and those mountains. Such beauty. And, at times, such ugliness down here. Like now.

"So, what's happening with you these days?" Sally asked, easing back in her chair.

Across the desk from her, Colton thought how beautiful this woman was.

Yet right now his attention was on the spectacular view behind out the window behind her.

His chair was positioned to allow a maximum view of the Rockies. Sally's office was on the tenth floor of the Cherry Tower, a building built mostly of glass.

Her particular suite of offices was on the northwest corner of the building. "Corner" for this building was a misnomer. The windows in her office rounded the building in one continuous line affording a wonderful view. All she had to do was swivel around in her chair to look out at the mountains and downtown Denver.

"I bet everyone comments on the view, right?"

"It's a great conversation starter, yes. And it helps

most people relax. They don't think they're in a doctor's office."

"And, for a few brief moments, they can forget about their own troubles, why they came to you in the first place, right?"

She laughed. "For a little while, yes."

And why are you here, Colton? she wondered. "Didn't they get your attention?" she asked, referring to the Rocky Mountains.

"You're right. And, for a few brief moments, even I forgot why I came."

She remained silent. He would start talking in a minute. Evidently, he was going to start later than some, but he would start.

It would not be the first thing he talked about, which she figured in his case could be police work. For most that came to her, it was not the first thing they brought up that was their problem. Most people did not get to their own problem until the third thing they mentioned. And then they did not even know or recognize that worry as being the source of all their problems. Most people thought the first thing they wanted to talk about was their problem since that was on their mind.

It was her job to get them to discuss that third item in such a way that they hardly knew they were. Sure, sometimes it took many hours of talking about the first two things, but often that third thing crept in while they thought they were talking out the other things.

He smiled at her. "Since most of your patients probably spend five or ten minutes talking about the mountains, I don't think I'm going to."

Her eyebrows shot up. "Oh, garrulous this afternoon, are we?"

"We?" he repeated. "If you feel like I do, you're in trouble."

"Oh? Want to talk about it?"

"No, I just thought I'd come and admire the view."

Once again, she remained silent. He really was in a particularly bad mood. He was usually so even-tempered.

She leaned forward, pushing a button on her telephone. "Hold any calls, please, until I let you know," she instructed the person who responded.

She leaned back again, waiting for him to talk.

"It's this damned serial killer thing," he began.

"Serial killer?" she asked. This was news to her. Department shrink, or not, she had not heard about this one.

"Sorry, no one knows about it. I'm not even sure I should be telling you. But you have to keep things quiet, don't you?"

She shrugged. "To a certain extent, yes."

"What do you mean, to a certain extent? Aren't you sworn to keep your patients' conversations confidential?"

"Of course. But what if you sat there and told me you knew who the killer was, it was your cousin Billy, or someone like that. You swore you saw him do it. Don't you think I have a moral obligation to let the chief of police know?"

"Do you? Would you?" Colton asked.

"Since I don't think that's the case with you, I promise not to tell."

"Why don't you think I know?" he asked.

"Because if you did, it would be all over *The Denver Post* and *Rocky Mountain News*. But what about a serial killer? I haven't heard about that."

It was his turn to shrug. "It's these overdoses. They no longer seem to be simple random ODs from different parts of the Metro area. It looks like someone is giving them bad dope. And the funny thing is, Jack was on to something about these cases. He had put two and two together, so to speak, and was going to tell me all about it. As it was, he told me and showed me some basic things he was seeing. But it wasn't enough to have any hard evidence. There was only a theory, and he was going to check it out. In fact, that's what I *know* he was doing in the lab last week when he was murdered. I can't tell anyone about what he thought, though, because it fits into a theory I have about what's happening. I can't tell anyone except you and Pete, of course."

He smiled at her and told her the same thing he told Pete.

"You're serious, aren't you?" she asked. "You really think someone from Arkansas is after you because of something that happened six years ago."

"You've been talking to Pete, I see. You don't believe me," he responded, as seriously as she had asked it.

"I'm more inclined to believe what you said one of the men said, that someone you were responsible for sending to prison has a girlfriend whose brother finally decided to get even with you, probably because the sister, the girlfriend, has not shut up since the whole thing happened."

"That's why I've asked you today whether you think certain tendencies, mental tendencies, can and do run in families."

"You think Tom went crazy because he saw some of the disappearances, then felt so guilty he couldn't handle it, then decided to kill you because of what you did to the killer. Just like that." She snapped her fingers.

"Stranger things have happened," he countered.

"No, not just like that," he argued. "I don't think it happened suddenly. I think it's taken him all these years of having everything running through his mind, repeatedly. Every time the events went through his mind, they changed, became distorted. They finally became something entirely different from what they were in the beginning. But they did become something he couldn't handle anymore."

"So, you don't really think this Tom is dead?"

"I don't know. That's what I've asked Dan to check out down there in Arkansas. I would like a copy of the death certificate, signed by a reputable doctor in the area. Then, and only then, I might, just might, believe it."

She was silent for a long moment.

Colton almost laughed when she made a teepee of the fingers of both hands and put them to her mouth, bowing her head slightly.

He did smile at her suddenly.

"What?" she asked. She had been deep in thought, not conscious of her actions.

"You just looked like the stereotype of a shrink. Or, at least the shrinks we see parodied on TV."

He made the hand gesture.

"Oh, sorry," she said, giggling. "You know, I've heard that about you." She was back to being a doctor.

"What have you heard?" he asked.

"I've heard that you have a certain…ability, it seems. Some say ESP, some say you're psychic at times. Most just agree that you seem to have a 'sixth' sense about things."

He waved his hand in the air, dismissing such rumors. "I just call them feelings at times. I have feelings about things, that's all. Instinct. Just like some people are judges of others, that sort of thing."

"I have a 'feeling' you're being modest about this, but that's all right." She smiled. "What bothers me is that you really think there's a danger to you and your family from some unknown source."

His eyebrows shot up when she said unknown. "I don't think it's unknown at all," he said.

"But you feel you're in danger," she repeated.

"Yes, definitely. Me. Abby. Marsha."

"Abby and Marsha?" she asked, incredulously. "When did they come into this?"

"They've always been there. Maybe not Marsha, so much, but Abby was definitely a part of the equation from the beginning."

"He's after both of you?"

"Yes," he answered simply.

He looked her straight in the eye. For several long seconds, they just looked at each other.

At last, she blinked. "What have you done about any of these feelings?"

"I've sent Marsha and Abby out of town, out of danger. I hope," he added.

"You *are* serious," she repeated.

"You don't think I should be. You think I'm wrong." It was a statement, not a question. He knew how all this sounded, especially to a psychiatrist.

"I think you've thrown a third joker into the deck and it just won't play." She grinned at her comparison.

"Well, we've started a thorough check of everyone I've even had the slightest contact with for the last two years that went to jail or prison. We're checking those that lost loved ones due to gunplay or were even wounded because of some action I was involved in, any arrests I've made. We're trying to pinpoint anyone who might have a motive for revenge against me. Real or imagined," he added.

"That's better," she responded. She had started nodding her head as he had talked. "That makes more sense than someone coming back from the grave. You need something you can touch."

She relaxed, leaned back in her chair.

Colton then reached into his jacket pocket, pulling out the last capsule he had left from Nancy's apartment.

He held it up in the air between his fingers so she could see it. "Then there's always this," he said.

"Which is?" she asked.

"The drug that has been killing each of the victims making up the spiral."

"You're kidding." She sat forward to get a better view. "How did you get it?" she said, asking the logical question.

He told her about Nancy, the only one not killed, thanks to the quick actions of the boyfriend.

"What is it?" she asked.

"Ah, that's part of the mystery, a big part of the mystery. I think it *is* the mystery. I think if we can find out what's in here, we'll have the killer."

"It's orange powder," she said, after taking it in her hand, turning it over and over. She even took it to her nose and smelled it. It smelled like oranges.

"Yes."

"What drug is orange?" she asked, a frown between her eyes. Then she thought of something and looked quickly up at Colton. "Who knows about this?"

She handed the capsule back to Colton, who placed it carefully back in a plastic bag and put it in his pocket.

"No one," he said. "No one, except you and me. Now. Jack knew."

"Jack knew," she repeated. "Jack knew. And you think that's why he was murdered."

Colton smiled. "You're quick. I mean I've always known how intelligent you were. You wouldn't be the department shrink if you didn't have a lot going for you. But thank you for catching on so quickly."

"I'm not sure I have 'caught on' as you call it. What I think you're saying is that whoever is making these capsules, giving them to addicts, killing these people to get your attention, somehow found out that Jack knew what

was in here and thought it could be traced back to him.
Or her—" she added.

"Or close to finding out," Colton interrupted.

She waved that away, not wanting to lose her train of
thought.

"—and this same person killed Jack because he knew
Jack was getting too close to the truth."

"That's basically it in a nutshell, yes."

"The person wasn't ready to be found out yet.
Right?" she asked.

"Right. It just wasn't time."

"'Cause he's not finished playing with you?" she
asked, a hint of skepticism creeping into her tone. "You
really are that important in all this?"

Colton chose to ignore her tone. He knew how this
sounded.

"Correct. But I'm ready to take it to him," he said.

"How?" she asked. "You don't even know who it is.
It helps to know who you're going after before you go."

"True."

"I'm sorry, I forget. You think you know, don't you?
This Tom?"

"Just a feeling," he said, grinning.

She thought of something else.

"You haven't told anyone else about this?" She
pointed to his pocket.

"Nope."

"Withholding evidence?" she asked.

"No, I gave one of the capsules to Jack, as the official police forensics expert. Jack analyzed it. He knew
something but told me he wanted to double-check everything he suspected. It was important enough that someone
killed him because of it. I know some of what Jack knew.
We both know that if I turn this in, it will just get buried
somewhere in the evidence room. It'll take forever, and I

do mean forever, to convince someone to analyze it, if I could convince anyone at all. How could I convince the chief this drug killed every one of those homeless men? You see, the evidence dissipates in the cadaver after a short while. That's what Jack knew and told me."

"Only you?" she asked.

"As far as I know, I'm the only one he told. He was just ready to write a report the next day after he was killed. He also had a notebook with all his findings written in it. He showed me that much. But there has to be at least one other person he either told—or this person overheard us talking."

"The killer?"

"Yes, or someone who repeated things to the killer, whether knowingly or unintentionally, not knowing he or she was talking to a killer."

"Any ideas? Besides the Arkansas one, I mean."

"Nope."

"What are you going to do with it?" She was referring to the capsule. "Only Jack knew that was what killed them. Don't the MEs have to keep notes and recordings as they go along with an autopsy? Shouldn't there be a recording or something about them somewhere?"

"Jack kept a personal notebook that was taken when he was murdered."

"Ah," she said. "And you're the only one who knows about that also, I suppose?"

"Actually, I think Marilyn did. But maybe not all he recorded in it, just the fact that he kept a personal notebook of his cases."

"His wife?"

"Yes."

"You think? But maybe not, maybe just you?" she argued. "Colton, you're asking me to believe that you and the chief medical examiner were such good friends that you were the only one he told about some important, maybe the only, evidence in a series of deaths. This evidence would classify these deaths as murders, not just random ODs." She shook her head. "Colton, what's wrong with this picture? Do you really think you're that important that he told you and only you about this without turning it in as evidence? A little filled with our own importance here, aren't we?"

He looked straight at her, his jaw set. "No, I don't see it that way. I was Jack's best friend. This 'evidence' he found in everybody he autopsied disappeared within a day of death, maybe even hours. It appeared as an orange hue or tinge to the lips and under the fingernails. It went away as the body decomposed further. I don't know all the particulars of physical decomposition and Jack didn't bother with telling me all that. I think he told me about this thing because I was his friend and when the tint went away, he no longer had any hard evidence he needed in order to prove what he had found. Who would believe him?"

"Who, indeed?" she asked.

He ignored her skepticism. "A few days ago, before he was killed he had shown me a tissue sample under the microscope. He said there was an unknown substance there he was going to check out as soon as he had time. He had some tissue samples on slides from each of the bodies. I saw them. They also disappeared when he was murdered."

"Along with his personal notebook? And no one else knows about them, either. Correct?"

"Apparently not. When one of the assistant MEs gave me an inventory of the lab, they were not listed on there or listed as missing. Nothing was listed as missing except the general notebook, in fact."

"You realize you've just thrown a couple more jokers into the deck? This is getting really far out, Colton. And weird, I might add."

"I know."

She decided to change the subject back to the third subject he had mentioned. "Jack," she said softly, watching him. "Tell me about Jack."

"What's to tell?" he asked, the hostility coming through his voice. He's dead."

"You need to talk about it," she said positively. She didn't ask him, she told him.

He needed to let the pain of losing such a good friend in such a way outside.

He hung his head.

He talked. He didn't stop for over an hour.

He leaned back in his chair, wiping his hands on his slacks.

"I didn't realize I hurt so much," he said.

"It's okay to hurt, to feel pain and sorrow. The harmful thing is that you try to keep it inside. Shared pain is a good cure. Have you talked to Marsha at all about Jack?"

"Oh, yeah," he said. "I don't think we stopped talking for two days."

"What does she think about your theory?"

"I haven't told her. You, Pete, and Jack are the only ones I've told."

She smiled. She couldn't help it. The first thing she had thought when she met Colton three years ago was she wished he wasn't married.

"Tendencies, maybe, toward craziness or madness that can be inherited? Can the genes of one malformed brain be passed down to another generation, causing someone down the line to do the same things?" he said, asking the question out of the blue.

"Certainly, there are family traits that are handed down from one generation to another," she began. "But

this sounds like more of an environmental thing that happened six years ago. You may not be aware of this, but I
am a strong environmentalist. I believe the area, the sur-
roundings, the teachings a person is exposed to from birth
to adulthood are the strongest deciding factors in how
that person believes and what he or she seems as normal
or conventional. You said this Tom, this friend of the
man you thought was the murderer, appeared to be perfectly normal to you."

She just threw it out to him as a statement. There was
no question. But she knew he would respond.

"What's normal to those people?" he asked. "Within
any area of the country, within any given set of people,
what is normal may take on a completely different meaning than someone else's normal. Besides, what if this
Tom went crazy with the knowledge that he was aiding
the murderer, as being the same as committing the crimes
himself? What if he just couldn't handle that and the
more he thought about it, the more it drove him insane?"

"You said he was dead. He can't be the one doing
the killings."

"Yeah, that's the only hang-up. Yet I wonder if he
really is dead?"

She looked very skeptical. "Can you find out for
sure?"

"Yeah, through my brother Dan I told you about. The
one who helped me back then. He's still the sheriff there.
In fact, he's supposed to call me back in a few days to let
me know more details about this whole story."

They were both silent for a few moments.

Colton sat with his arms on his knees, leaning forward. He wasn't thinking of anything in particular. It
seemed that talking for so long had completely drained
him.

"All you have to do now is tie all this together and get real proof, hard evidence, right?"

He looked up at her. "Right. That's all. Simple, right?" He shook his head, standing up. "Thanks for letting me yak at you like this. Since it's a personal thing, just send me a bill, okay? I don't want the chief of police getting a bill for this time and questioning me about why and who and how. You know what I mean. I certainly don't want to give him any reason to pull me off these ODs. And he certainly wouldn't be very sympathetic to my theories. In fact, no one here in Denver knows about the thing six years ago in Arkansas. Well, Pete. And Jack knew, but no one else did. Now you—hell, yes, Jack *knew*."

He looked at her as if something had just occurred to him, some idea. "That's just another reason to add to all the other reasons of why he could have been killed. He knew about that because I had told him. He asked me in the parking lot of the hospital that day what all I knew about the family of the malformed kid in Arkansas. He was starting to tie something in, just like I am."

Colton paced back and forth across Sally's office, running his fingers through his hair, pointing at the air as he talked. "The more I think about it, the more I'm convinced that someone overheard us talking in the hospital parking lot. I just wish I could remember who all was around us."

"You're beating yourself to death with that one," she admonished him. "How can you expect to remember everyone coming and going in a busy hospital parking lot during the day? You have family and friends of the patients, you have hospital workers, vendors, and lots of other people. Unless someone was dressed up in a clown suit or had a pink Cadillac or something that would stand out like that, there's no way you can remember every-thing. Not even a super cop like you."

She tried to make the situation lighter, but it didn't work.

"We're trained to see, remember?"

He was really down on himself. She suggested he come back in two days for another session. He just wasn't letting go of Jack. He was almost blaming himself for Jack's murder, and there was no way at all he could have foreseen it. It seemed a real wild card, in light of all the others.

She wasn't convinced his theory of what was happening was very plausible, but Colton was convinced. And she hoped that just might be enough to spur him on to find the killer.

Chapter 30

"Colton," the chief of police called.

Colton did an about-face. He'd been headed in the opposite direction but started working his way through the maze of desks and chairs to the chief of police's office.

The chief stepped back, allowing Colton to enter the room. Then he shut the door.

That held a certain significance. When the chief of police shut the door, things were critical.

"Coffee?" he asked Colton.

Colton walked over to the Mr. Coffee machine. He helped himself to a cup of the chief's own blend. It was strong enough to kill a horse. But Colton decided that was exactly what he needed—something strong enough to keep him alert.

When he turned back from the coffeepot, he nodded to the other man already seated in the room with the chief. "Richard," Colton acknowledged.

"Morning," the other man responded.

"Well, as long as you didn't say 'good morning,' that's okay, then," Colton said. "Good, it ain't been."

"How is Marilyn?" the chief asked.

He could be very hard-nosed when he needed to be, sometimes downright ruthless, but Colton had always given him credit for being genuinely interested in and concerned about his men. He looked as if he had lost a good friend in Jack, also.

Colton shrugged. "I called her mom and sister to come to her house and be with her. I just couldn't bring myself to tell her what really happened. I told her simply that he had been killed in the lab, in the line of duty. She questioned how he could be killed that way, but seemed satisfied when I said it was an apparent robbery. I stayed until her sister got there, then came back here." He sighed. "At some point, of course, she's going to have to be told the truth of how he died. I don't know if I can do it."

"What about the priest?" Richard asked.

Richard was another detective on the same level with Colton. There had never been any jealousy between them. Both men had strong egos and self-esteem. They knew what both and each could do and had carried out different assignments with intelligence and efficiency.

They had a mutual respect and liking for each other.

"Probably end up with him, you know that," Colton said. "He'll probably want to talk with me, also. I was there. I can tell her as much or as little as I want to. Later."

Both men looked at the chief of police expectantly as they drank their coffee. They knew they had been called in there for a reason.

Since Colton was already officially on the case of the "serial killer," he assumed they were going to be told Richard had been put in charge of investigating Jack's murder. Colton usually started them, and someone stepped in.

He was right. Since it involved still using some of his

men, though, Colton had to be informed. Richard was going to take over Jack's case. The chief of police felt that Colton was too emotionally involved.

Colton told Richard what he had seen and heard. He could tell by the look in Richard's eyes that he still didn't want to believe him. Colton had invited him to go to the morgue to see for himself.

"Any suggestions on this for me?" Richard asked Colton, since Colton had been there and would be the one writing the initial report of the scene.

"Before I do a detailed report, all I can tell you is that it looks like an apparent robbery, maybe by someone on speed or crack. Something. I've started the men on checking out old files. Maybe they can find anyone who might have had a personal vendetta against him, even from years ago. Also, one of the assistants checked out the inventory as soon as the place was cleaned up. Forensics will take a while longer, of course. But what someone wanted to steal is beyond me."

Colton could not tell him what was missing. They would have immediately sent him back to Sally.

"Satanic ritual?" Richard suggested.

"I thought of that," Colton admitted. He shrugged. "Who knows? It sounds just as good as anything else, doesn't it? Makes just as much sense. I don't know. I just don't know." He rubbed his forehead and did circles around his temples with his fingers. His head felt like it would explode. "By the way, I thought you were on vacation," he said to Richard. The thought had just occurred to him.

"We were," Richard admitted. "We got home last night. I refused to listen to any messages until this morning. Late. My plans were to sleep in, and I did. I'll take the next few days another time. I want to catch this guy, probably as much as you do."

No, you don't, Colton thought, *for reasons you would never understand.*

Chapter 31

A week had gone by, and Colton still had not heard from Dan. That was unusual. Dan usually got right on to something and got it done.

Colton called him. If the chief asked about the call, he could pay for it himself. Some things were just important, even if they couldn't be explained.

Or believed.

"South Sebastian County Sheriff's Office."

The voice sounded familiar, but Colton couldn't quite place it. "May I speak to Dan, please," he requested. He used his most professional voice.

The voice hesitated. "Uh…Dan…"

"Yes, Dan. You know, the sheriff."

What was this? Had there been an election that Dan had failed to mention and he had been voted out of office? Nah, not Dan. He was too good and too popular with the people.

Colton knew he hadn't called a wrong number. The department had acknowledged.

Why did he have a bad feeling about this?

"I'm sorry, but the sheriff…uh…Dan…was hurt in a

car accident last night. He's in the hospital in critical condition. Who is this?" the deputy thought to ask.

Dan? Hurt? In a car wreck? "Are you sure?" was all Colton could manage. What a dumb question.

"Am I sure? Who is this?" the deputy repeated. His voice had changed. Of course, the man was sure his boss was in the hospital.

"Name's Colton Mitchell. I am—er—was—a friend of Dan's. *Am* a friend—brother," he corrected.

"Colton! Why didn't you say so? This is Frank. You were next on my list to call about Dan. I wasn't looking forward to calling you, I might say."

"Frank." No wonder the voice had sounded familiar. This was the deputy that had helped them the most six years ago. "Frank," Colton repeated. "What happened? You said last night?"

"Yeah. On a hill just south of here, coming back this way from Midland. It's a bad stretch of road. There've been a couple of wrecks along there through the years. Roads were damp from a rain we'd had. And you probably don't know about these Arkansas highways when they get even a little damp. They can really be hell in bad weather. People hydroplane a lot. He just lost control, the best we can figure it. Maybe a rabbit, dog, cat, whatever jumped out in front of him and he over-compensated and with the wet road—who knows? Some deep shoulder clumping seems to point to his losing control, over compensating, trying to get back on the pavement.

"Unfortunately, there's about a half-inch drop-off onto the shoulder along there. And there are signs up warning of a rough shoulder."

"Dan knew that. He knew how to drive on those roads," Colton said, stating it as a fact rather than a question.

"Oh, yeah, sure," Frank replied. "That's why we

think he was faced with a sudden emergency, lost control. Then he ran into the bridge guardrail at the bottom of the hill, flipped over, and went down the embankment. At first glance, it looked as if he was dead, but he groaned, and the first responders knew he was alive, just unconscious. If that helps," he added then continued. "Fortunately, another car came along just then and saw Dan's car take the plunge. Now, he's in a coma. Doctors don't know when he'll come out of it."

"Thank God for that much," Colton agreed. But he still couldn't believe his brother was in a coma.

His mind was racing. Last night. Coming back from Midland.

Now, what was the significance of that? Was there any? It was right on the tip of his tongue, but he couldn't remember.

Too tired.

Yeah, too tired of this whole damned business.

"Frank, did anyone check the patrol car for tampering, that sort of thing?"

"Why, no," the deputy said. He seemed surprised that Colton would ask such a thing. "It was just an accident."

"Somehow, I don't think so, but I can't talk about it on the phone. Do you still have the vehicle?"

"Sure, it's in impound. We have to keep it for a certain time."

Probably for just this sort of thing, you just don't know it, Colton thought.

"Do me and your department a favor and have your mechanic check it out, okay? Look for cut brake lines, that sort of thing. Your mechanic will know what to look for. I'll be there tomorrow, and I'll explain everything."

Colton swirled his chair around and looked out this window. He saw nothing.

His mind couldn't put a coherent thought together. Although he knew accidents happened, his instincts also told him this was no accident.

First the homeless.

Then Jack.

Now Dan was in a coma from a car crash, which Colton knew was no accident. He shuddered.

Was someone walking across his grave?

Chapter 32

It came to him as suddenly as Jack's letters had.

There was one call on the list of the phone calls from Midland to Denver that made his blood run cold. A call had come to Denver the day before Dan had been hurt in his "accident."

Accident, my ass, thought Colton.

But the only thing that would happen to his ass was that the chief would chew on it if Colton took such "evidence" to him.

Colton was completely on his own with this.

He booked a flight to Arkansas.

After the captain of the airplane had finished welcoming the passengers to the friendly skies, Colton put his seat back and turned off the overhead light.

It had taken quite a bit of talking to convince the chief to let him make the trip, but, in the end, he had agreed. *Probably the offer of paying my own way,* Colton thought.

But he had to admit the chief wasn't really like that. He just couldn't justify one of his best men taking a flight of fancy right in the middle of a homicide investigation, or at least what the chief felt was nonsense. He told Colton in no uncertain terms what he thought about this "wild-goose chase."

"Ever been snipe hunting, Mitchell?" he'd asked, shaking his head.

"No such thing," Colton had replied.

"Exactly," was the chief's reply.

"Well, what is it, Chief? Wild geese or snipes?"

Colton had the good sense to leave the office as the chief's face turned a bright red.

Now, on board the flight, he yawned for a while, then slept.

He did not wake up until the plane set down in Fort Smith, Arkansas. He was lucky this particular airline had a non-stop flight, since it was not a major airport.

His rental car was ready, and he was soon speeding down Highway 71 toward Midland. Fortunately, the airport was on the south side of town, so he was out of heavy traffic quickly.

The drive brought back memories of six years before. He had first driven down this road on what he thought was just a trip for nostalgia's sake, an "auld lang syne" type of thing. His vacation at the time had quickly become a nightmare as he worked frantically to solve an age-old mystery of who had been kidnapping children over a twenty-year period. When he found out his daughter was missing his search became an all-consuming one. He had not known he even had a daughter, his Abby, until he arrived in Midland those six years ago. His high school sweetheart had never told him she was pregnant. With the help of a local elder and a newfound friend Colton was able to rescue his daughter. She was the next intended victim of the kidnapper/murderer. They had been forced to kill the murderer. Now, it seemed these murders in Denver were somehow connected to that event.

He first wanted to visit Tom's place. He wanted to talk to the people who had bought it.

But even before he went to Tom's, he wanted to "cruise" through his hometown once again. After all, it had been six years, and he didn't know when he would be back again. The trip through town *migh*t take ten minutes.

Tops.

Chapter 33

Reduced Speed Ahead, forty-five to thirty-five to twenty-five.

Colton turned slowly onto Main Street, Midland. Even at first glance, he had all the same thoughts and memories of six years ago.

The first building he came to was the old general store, once advertising *GENERAL MERCHANDISE AND DRY GOODS* on its side. There were still traces of the letters, but perhaps you would recognize them only if you knew they were once there. It still had the front porch the length of the building, with wide, plate-glass windows. The double glass front door was still in place, down to the original hand-beveled glass.

The building was still in use. To Colton, the visible signs of life were the three rocking chairs spread across the front porch, two of them on either side of a barrel with a checkerboard on top of it.

He wondered if any of the men in town still played. When he was a boy, as soon as one man got up, having his fill of checkers or probably having lost too many games, another was ready to take his place, hoping to defeat whoever was reigning champion of that day. There had been an unwritten rule: whoever won the most games that day got his evening mug of beer paid for by the others. So, a game was always in progress.

Of course, back then there were still plenty of men in town to keep a game going.

The general store was a free-standing building and the next block started a row of businesses. By the look of them now, most of them had been closed for years.

But Colton remembered what had occupied each space. The store on the corner, the one where the double doors faced the corner, had been the tobacco shop.

He had never been allowed to go in there, the proprietors then having had a more moral sense of responsibility than some did now. And the young Colton made sure he parked his bicycle around the corner, down the side, off Main Street, so he could have every opportunity to amble slowly past the open doors, taking slow, deep breaths.

The smell of the various tobaccos was heavenly to a boy, who dreamed of smoking a pipe and wearing a fancy smoking jacket like he saw on TV. That would make him rich, or that's how it appeared.

Colton could imagine the smells as he drove by.

Next to the tobacco shop had been the candy store. Mrs. Little also had a doll collection, which attracted the girls. The candy store was his excuse to go past the tobacco shop with its wonderful odors, to buy a nickel's worth of candy was all he needed to tease some girl and pull her pigtail. And there was always a girl in there, or so it seemed.

Mrs. Little would scold him and tell him to "shoo," but he always managed to hang around a little while.

Now that third store was a beauty shop, Kate's Kut 'N Kurl, and there were two cars parked out front.

The next store front displayed a hand-painted

"Crafts" on the window. Although there did appear to be a few items in the windows, the sign on the door said "closed."

Colton wondered if that meant this store wasn't open for business yet that day since it was very early, or if it were permanently closed.

Across the street had been the biggest grocery store in town. It was now closed, but the old metal Coca-Cola machine was still on the front porch.

Colton remembered running across the street from the candy store, putting his other nickel in the slot and pulling the glass bottle across and up. If no one else was around, he had a hard time opening, holding up the heavy lid, and sliding the Coca-Cola across and up at the same time.

But he would never forget the taste of those Cokes! Sometimes he only got a dime to spend, so it was a real treat. He would nurse it as long as possible. There were times, instead of candy, he would buy a bag of peanuts, drink the Coca-Cola down a little, then empty the bag into the bottle. It was the best way to eat peanuts and drink a Coke.

Next to the grocery store was the newspaper office. By the looks of things, it had also long since closed. There was a time when no one went without a *Midland Weekly*. He could picture his mother pouring over the gossip columns and "tsk-tsking" at some tidbit or other. Of course, the ladies who submitted the columns, even from the outlying communities, would never have admitted it was gossip, but rather items of interest to the community. Besides, didn't everyone like to see their name in print?

A newspaper stand containing the *Southwest Times-Record*, a Fort Smith paper, now stood on the sidewalk.

From the lack of businesses open in town, Colton

thought he could figure out why the *Midland Weekly* had stopped publishing.

Unfortunately, now, six years later, the hardware/feed store had closed. By the looks of the building, it had been boarded up for several years. There were no more hoes, shovels, pic-axes, or whatever standing up in a barrel on the front porch. At one time, the owner was getting quite elderly, so maybe it was just a matter of his getting too old to run the store and no one else wanted to. Colton, suspected, however, that there was simply no more business. With Wal-Mart, Lowe's, Ace Hardware, and other competitors in Fort Smith, why should anyone with need of such pay higher prices? Chances were, they went into Fort Smith for other supplies, anyway.

Another mom-and-pop bit the dust.

The next block was barren, but the sidewalk and old fire hydrant were still there. The old town library building was long since gone.

Almost as quickly, then Colton was through Main Street, turning right, down between rows of houses.

Maple Street, where he used to live. Yes, the house was there, lived in by strangers, since his parents had moved to Fort Spenser some years before. Colton pulled to a stop at the side of the street, reminiscing. He could almost see himself flying out of the front door, taking the steps two by two, running down the sidewalk, and then down the street, his dog beside him all the way.

After driving slowly up and down several streets, slowing even more, to look at old friends' houses and the ball park, Colton decided to go back to the general store. That's where he would find out what was happening to the town.

Colton remembered that if it had not been for the gibberish of Old Man Ogden, he would never have been able to put the clues together as to the possible location of the kidnapper/murderer/whatever you wanted to call the "thing" that had taken seven girls and boys over those past twenty years.

Also, he would not have known that he had a daughter. So, really, he had a lot to be thankful to Old Man Ogden for, and the old man would probably never know.

As he drove slowly through town, so many memories came flooding over him. Memories of his childhood, finding Marsha, then learning that Abby was his daughter, but she was missing, just about to the date that all the other children had "gone missing."

He was happy to see so many dogs and cats in town. On one street, he had to carefully and slowly maneuver around a large dog lying asleep in almost the middle of the street. The dog simply never woke up or moved.

Colton stopped beside it and watched it for a few seconds to make sure its side was moving, that it was alive, before he carefully drove on. He smiled and shook his head.

After all, there was a time when there were *no* dogs or cats in this town.

⁰⁵⁰⁵⁰

When he pulled into the dirt driveway, two hound dogs raised their heads to look at the car and at him as he emerged. Then they simply lowered their heads again, one rolling onto its side. It was too hot to bark, let alone move. Colton thought of the expression "lickin' pot hound" and decided these were such dogs.

"Hello," Colton called out.

Experience had taught him not to get too close. He stood beside the car. The right screen door of the house opened, and a big, burly man stepped out onto the porch. A frail-looking woman and a scraggly-haired girl of about six years old followed him. "Howdy, neighbor," the man said by way of greeting.

Good, Colton thought. *A friendly native.* "Good morning," he replied.

He identified himself and asked about Otis, Tom, and Tom's wife.

"Hey, you the guy who killed the monster what was killing those little girls?" the man asked.

Colton was impressed. "That's me, but I had help."

"Just glad you did," the man said, nodding over toward the little girl. "Hey, come on up and take a load off."

The man gestured to one of the chairs on the porch and Colton took the three steps up to the porch. He lowered himself slowly into a cane-backed chair. He wasn't sure the chair would support him. Although it gave several squeaks and groans as he settled into it, it did seem strong enough.

He relaxed.

The woman had disappeared back into the house. The little girl sat at the other end of the porch and played with a doll.

Colton accepted a glass of tea from the woman. "How long have you lived here?" he asked the man.

"'Bout three months," was the reply. "Bought it off Tom's wife. She needed to sell after Tom died. Didn't have much income, poor thing, needed some money."

Poor thing? Colton wondered, glancing around. Could these people actually pity someone worse off than they were? Was there anyone poorer?

"Do you know where she moved to?" Colton asked.

The man pushed his hat back and scratched his head, still holding on to his hat. "Don't rightly know," he said. "Only, seems I remember hearing something about West Virginia. Family or something. Maybe she went there.

She was a quiet one, she was. Never hardly said a word."

"She was a Schnook," the woman said, speaking for the first time.

"She were?" the man asked, looking over at his wife in surprise. "You never told me that."

She shrugged. "No need to," she said. "You ever sick?"

"Well, no," he said, unconsciously puffing his chest out. "Can't say I ever am."

"Well?" she asked.

"Right," he agreed.

Colton had lost the conversation. "What's a shook?" he asked.

"Not a shook, a S-c-h-o-o-k," she said patiently, spelling the name. "And it's not a what, it's a who."

"Then, who?" he asked.

"Ain't you never heard of the Schnooks?" the man asked, taking a long gulp of his tea.

"Can't say that I have," Colton replied.

Funny. He found himself starting to talk like these people.

The woman just shook her. "The Schnooks were, are, a famous family. Started in West Virginia a couple hundred years ago but some of 'em wondered this way over the years, across Kentucky and Tennessee. Maude was the last of the line. It really weighed heavily on her, too, bless her soul. What a burden. No one to pass the family's secrets down to."

"What secrets?" Colton asked quickly, before the woman could take a breath and continue her spiel.

"You just don't know anything, do you?" the man asked.

"Hush, Jeremy, 'course he don't. City slicker ain't expected to know. Be polite, now."

"Yes, ma'am," he returned quietly.

"Guess I don't know much about these parts," Colton agreed. There he was, talking like them again.

"The Schnooks knew every root, every stem, every flower and berry in the forest," Jeremy said. "They could take just about any herb or spice, anything from the forest, and cure someone with it. Just about anything that ailed you, too. How they mixed 'em, what they were, and what part this or what part that was their secret. And they wouldn't share. They were well-known healers—"

"Maude didn't do much herself, though," the wife interrupted. "She knew all the plants and things, but she didn't let anyone know she did. Just weren't her way."

"If her knowledge was going to die with her, why didn't she pass it on to someone? You seem to have known her, why couldn't she have told you rather than let all the secrets die out?" Colton asked.

"Oh, no, she couldn't do that. I ain't family."

"Then how'd you know she were a Schnook?" her husband asked. He seemed to find this newfound secret about his wife amazing. He was truly impressed with her.

"She told me," the woman replied.

"Just told you? Hell, woman, do you believe everything you're told?" Jeremy was suddenly angry with her.

"Hold on, Jeremy," she said, reaching over and patting his arm. "Remember when I was carrying young Mary there and started bleeding? Almost lost her?"

"Yeah," he agreed.

"Remember when Maude came to visit? Came right into the bedroom, she did, just to see me."

"Yeah?"

"Remember that bag she always carried?"

"Yeah?" the man was getting impatient.

Colton found himself on the edge of his chair waiting for the story to unfold.

"She gave me something that night. Made me take it.

Left me some to take for several days. Told me it would save the baby. By the next day, I quit bleeding. She came back that next night, and I knew. Don't ask me how, I just did. I looked her straight in the eye, I did, just as bold as punch and said, 'you're a Schnook.' She just nodded. Didn't lose her, did I?" she asked, nodding toward the little girl. "In fact, that very week I was up cooking your meals. Remember?"

He nodded.

"Was her recipe that saved Mary."

"Why didn't you tell anyone?" he asked.

"Weren't mine to tell, and, besides, she asked me not to. Said she was the last one. She was right ashamed of that. Seems only the females in line could have the secrets passed on to them. Tom and her only had the one boy. She felt ashamed she never had a girl to pass her knowledge down to."

They *did* have a son.

Colton sat up at that. "You say only girls could carry on the healing line?"

"Seems so."

"Any chance she might have taught things to her boy, that's why she never told anyone who she was? Maybe she broke an old, time-honored tradition, did something taboo. Maybe then she felt she couldn't tell," Colton said.

They were all silent, weighing what he had said.

"Could be, I reckon," the woman said at last. "Just could be. I hadn't thought of that. Wouldn't be right, though."

"Could he learn any less because he was male instead of female?" Colton asked gently.

"No—o—o, 'course not," was the long, drawn-out reply. "Just wouldn't be right."

"But—" Jeremy began then stopped.

"But, what?" Colton asked.

"Well, when we bought the place, the son was living here," the woman continued. "He asked us if he could leave some things in one of the shanties out back, the farthest one, for a while, 'til he got his mama settled. We said sure, of course. Told us if he weren't back for the things within a year, just break the padlock off the door and clean the shanty out for ourselves. We didn't need the space, so it was okay with us. Came back about three…six…months ago and got the things out. Carried out box after box of something."

"Sounded like jars rattling against each other," the man supplied. "Probably his mother's canning. Never saw what it was, though."

"I did," a small voice said, speaking up for the first time.

All three of them looked toward the end of the porch where the little girl, Mary, was still playing with her doll.

"What did you say, honey?" her mother asked.

"I did."

"You did what?"

"Saw what he had in the boxes. He didn't know I saw, but I did."

"How did you see, Mary?"

The little girl was silent. She had been taught not to spy on people.

It seems like the talent for not telling anything has been passed down in this family, Colton thought. "You won't be in trouble if you tell us."

She looked at her dad with a question in her eyes.

"It's okay," her father said.

"I climbed up on those boxes that are stacked up behind that shed. Looked right through the window."

The parents nodded, agreeing. They knew what she was talking about. It was possible.

"And what did you see?"

"Lots of jars. Most full of weeds and sticks and grass."

The three adults were silent.

Was the little girl making up a story?

"Honey, are you sure it weren't canned tomatoes or peaches or green beans or something like that in the jars?" her mom asked gently.

"Nope. Weeds and sticks."

Finally, the woman spoke. "Then maybe she did teach him. Or maybe he just came back for her stuff and was taking it to her."

"What was it?" Colton asked, intrigued.

"It looked like weeds and sticks to a little girl but those would have been her roots and berries, herbs, and spices for her remedies. Jars are the best way to keep them dry, keep flavor and properties in."

"I'd say you're right," the husband agreed.

"He came back for them because they were that important to her. So, he came back. Being a good son," the woman said.

"Do you know where he lives now?" Colton asked.

"Can't rightly say. West Virginia, I guess. Although she was the last of the healing line, she could've had cousins and uncles and aunts somewhere. And the boy would take care of her. She was…" The woman started to say something then stopped.

"Was what?" Colton asked quietly.

"Well, some say she was slightly off."

"Off?" Colton asked, not understanding.

"Goofy. Crazy," the man said.

"Jeremy. Them's harsh words."

"Well, true, anyway."

"Maybe, maybe not. But you know we're trying to teach Mary not to call people things like that."

Jeremy managed to look sheepish. "Sorry," he apologized.

But when the wife looked over to see if Mary had been listening, Jeremy drew a circle in the air around his temple with his index finger, the universal sign for crazy.

"But you don't know for sure where I could find them?" Colton asked again. He hoped they had thought of something.

They hadn't. In a few minutes, Colton stood, thanked her for the tea, and left.

It seemed a dead end.

The woman and her young son had gone back to who knew where.

Chapter 34

Colton stopped at the general store in Midland. Strange. Six years ago, it had not changed from when he was a boy growing up here. Now, six years later, it had changed in the way of another store or two closing.

He shook his head. Life seemed to stand still in this small town.

Marsha made several trips a year here to visit with her parents, but Colton usually had some case that needed his attention. He had come back a few times but did not do the same "nostalgia" trip he had six years ago. He hadn't needed that since.

With Mr. Adams gone, the store was different in a way that you could not put your finger on. His grandson managed it now. When asked, he said Otis and Tom used to come and go but, what with Otis in the institution now and Tom moved away, there wasn't anyone who came to "sit a spell."

Locals just came and went. There were now two public phone booths in Midland. One of them was on the porch of the general store. The number checked out with the one from Jennie's report.

What did that prove, though?

It proved jack, Colton thought.

He used the expression without thinking about it, but it made him think of Jack's death. But calls from one pay phone to another pay phone proved nothing. The calls could even have been from a tourist who had stopped in this small town.

Although Colton knew differently, *intuition* was not acceptable enough evidence to take to the chief. But, who did Tom know in Denver?

Of course, they would only find the answer to that when, and if, they found the killer. Alive.

Colton used this same phone booth to call back to Denver.

Marsha had taken several messages for him. The most important to him was one that she almost forgot to tell him about.

"Oh, wait," she said, as he started to hang up.

"What?" he asked.

"Do you know a Dr. Langier?"

"Langier? Langier? I can't say that I do. Who is he?"

"I don't know. He called from some universi-ty…here it is—"

"Oh, yes, yes," Colton interrupted.

He had given up on hearing about the tissue and cap-sule had sent to the professor at the research department of the University of West Virginia. He only knew the vial had been received because the green card for certified mail had come back to him.

"What did he say?"

"You want it over the phone? The message was so long that I asked him to fax it to me. Can you get to a fax machine and call me back? I'll send it to you."

"Yeah. I'll go to Dan's office. Stay by the phone, okay? It'll take me at least thirty minutes to get there.

"I'll be here. We miss you."

After assuring her he missed them and loved them, he started north on Highway 256 to Dan's office in Greenwood. He would swing across to Highway 70 at Hackett.

The report was the proverbial "good news, bad news," situation, at least to the professor.

It began: *Commander Mitchell, let me apologize for not getting back to you until now. I had taken a few days of leave when your package arrived. This is very exciting. What you sent me was put through every test we have here. The tissue contained plant microbes, but I have never seen this particular microbe. Do you have more? It produces an unknown substance, briefly, one that is orange in color. We would like to do research on it, especially in light of its history of imitating a drug overdose then dissipating so it cannot be detected. The nearest thing I could find to it is a plant called Nightshade. Deadly Nightshade is also called Belladona—*

"Belladona! Belladona!" Colton said to Frank, the deputy on duty. "What is that? What is it?" He was very excited. He knew he was on to something here, something just outside his grasp. Then it hit him. *Fair lady! That's it. The pusher called Nancy 'fair lady.' Now, how did I even remember that?*

He was getting more excited by the moment.

The report went on: *...the dried leaves and roots of Atropa belladonna...*

Colton laughed again, glancing up at Frank. "Look," he said, pointing to the scientific name, *Atropa belladona.* "Abd."

"What?" Frank asked. "What is it?"

"Abd. I'll be damned. Those are the letters Jack wrote in his notebook. I was right. We just didn't look far enough or have the right books for detail. I can't believe it."

He looked back at the report.

...and roots of Atropa belladona, the active principal of which is atrophine. Poisoning from atrophine is attended by extreme dryness of mouth and throat, due to paralysis of the chorda tympani nerve which diminishes supply of saliva; huskiness of the voice, redness of tongue, great thirst, difficulty in swallowing and marked dilation of the pupils making the eyes prominent, brilliant, staring and interfering with accommodation of the eye, making rear vision difficult or impossible. Distant vision is unimpaired. Hallucinations, dizziness, vertigo, excitement, and delirium are usually present. The patient may be violent or merely hilarious. Nausea is common, the pulse is at first strong but later becomes weak and rapid or even imperceptible. The skin is dry and may be hot. These symptoms may come on in susceptible patients when the drug is given in ordinary dosage but an excessive amount is usually required. Commander, please refer to the accompanying pamphlet from the West Virginia Department of Agriculture. It lists other characteristics of Nightshade.

"West Virginia! West Virginia!" Colton exclaimed. "I knew it. I just knew it. It all ties in."

The report continued. *But I must remind you that this is a virulent mutation of Nightshade. It is much more aggressive. It probably did not take much of this to cause a severe reaction. Need I urge you to find the source of this*

*drug and eliminate it as a drug for the streets? When you
find the source, please do not destroy the plants. Please
send them to us. We do want to study them. Please let me
know if this has been helpful to you.*

Helpful? *Helpful?*

The professor would never, in his lifetime, even
begin to imagine how helpful he had been. Nor would he
ever believe Colton if he tried to explain.

"Are you going to tell me what this is all about, or
what?" Frank asked. "What's West Virginia got to do
with Tom? And what's Tom got to do with anything in
West Virginia? He's dead."

"No, I don't think so," Colton replied. "I think
Tom's alive and well and that's why I have to go to West
Virginia. I need to call the airport for flight schedules,
then I'll tell you all about it if I have time."

Colton found a connecting flight to Charleston, the
capital of West Virginia, the next afternoon. That was
good. He could visit the genealogy section of the main
library, trace the Schnook family line, and be on his way
before dark.

ↃↄↃↄ

Colton took time the next morning to check on Dan
in the hospital but knew there was nothing he could do
for him at this point. Then he had lunch with a couple of
the deputies and told them everything. They were certainly more willing to accept the theory than were his co-
workers in Denver.

But, then, they had both been here six years ago.
Over lunch, they heard the whole story of the overdoses,
the orange tint that Jack had discovered, the orange candy
that Abby had become addicted to, Jack's death—

everything. Colton told them his theory and why he thought everything was connected to Tom, especially considering what Dan himself had told him.

They believed him and trusted his instincts. They had seen Colton in action before. Hadn't he been the one to know something was in the Old Spenser House six years ago? They just hoped he was right.

And that still did not solve the problem of finding Tom before he killed again or decided to end his "game" and harm Colton or Abby.

Chapter 35

est Virginia was beautiful country. Colton certainly had to give it that. They flew into
Charleston with the sun reflecting off the gold
dome of the state capitol building. What a sight to see.

There were very few state capitol buildings with gold
like that and Charleston was one of them. Denver was
another. Yet the two were vastly different.

After checking with the genealogical section at the
main library, he rented a car.

He drove the last ten miles of his journey between
the walls of a narrow valley. The glow of the sun seen off
the bushes provided a blaze of color, changing like a ka-
leidoscope every few feet. Flashes of orange, red, purple,
and yellow filled his senses.

How beautiful, he thought. *Is it like this every day or
is it happening just for me?*

He drove down the mountain range into a valley. A
river ran on one side of the valley. A two-lane highway
was on the other side. Occasionally a crude board house
would appear on the other side of the river, seemingly
built into the steep mountain.

How do they build there like that? he wondered.

He started watching closely, or as well as he could and still stay on the road. The next house he saw was almost a cabin. He slowed down to see it better.

It was made of rough-hewn logs chinked with mud. It could not be any bigger than two rooms. Maybe that window in the end on the second floor meant there was bedroom there. A sleeping room or loft, maybe. There was an attempt at a flowerbed out front, though, so someone lived here and cared.

Then he noticed something he had not before because of the slight mist off the mountains. Smoke curled lazily from a chimney near the middle of the building. Yes, they already needed a fire in these mountains although it was only September.

Were those clumps of snow in the shadows? Soon enough snow would fall in these mountains that some of the people would not be able to get out of their homes.

He was steadily climbing a mountain. The mid-sized car he had rented in Charleston had labored a couple of times during the trip. Now, he wondered if he would make it. He climbed up and up, encountering switchback after switchback. Just when he thought there was no top to this mountain, he was there.

He braked, almost too hard. He skidded a few feet in the loose gravel at the side of the road. He stopped at a pullover.

Had this place been formed out of necessity for those cars too hot by the time they reached the top or was it because of the sheer beauty of the scene below him? He wanted to believe the beauty was the reason, but he knew it probably wasn't so. The locals were probably so used to this landscape they never saw it anymore.

The same brilliant sun was shining upon the valley below that had lit his way through the previous narrow valley. The river still flowed in the valley, but there were houses on each side. In some spots, the houses went two and three streets deep.

Roofs reflected the sun. It bounced off the water, rippling like little diamonds up and down. He could see people moving around yet they were the size of ants from this distance.

Colton realized he was holding his breath and he let it out slowly. It was so quiet in this spot he thought he could hear his heart beating.

In the next second, however, the all-too-familiar sound of a truck laboring up the mountain ripped through the silence.

Better get going, he thought. *Don't want to argue with a log truck in these mountains, either coming or going.*

He had seen many flatbed trailers along the way, each laden with huge, long logs. Lumber was a way of life here. Either that or coal mining. But he didn't want to end up under a pile of the logs if a driver's brakes failed.

He drove down through more switchbacks, but the journey down seemed tame compared to the way up.

At the outskirts of a small community, a simple sign read "Branch Hollow." It was not a regular population or elevation sign, just a single line.

He stopped at a small store on the right side of the road. This was still a mom-and-pop store. It bore no resemblance whatsoever to the modern Texaco or Love's stations along the interstates or even in large cities.

Large plate glass windows on either side of a single door boasted posters of church socials, 4-H clubs, and school events. Some were outdated but had not been removed. Some were yellow with age.

Two gas pumps were out front with a narrow space between the building and the pumps through which to drive and park at the pumps. The driveway on the outer side of the pumps was not much larger. Colton stopped at the side of the building where tires were piled high. A sign declared "used tires for sale." Another hand-painted sign solicited "flats fixed." That seemed appropriate somehow.

Colton had the dumb thought that the pile must be the flats with holes in them.

As he went through the door, a bell attached to the door let the owners know someone was here.

"Howdy." A man greeted Colton as he came through the door. The man was wiping his greased-stained hands on a towel that didn't look any less dirty than his hands. "What can I do you for?"

He was friendly and willing to be helpful to this stranger.

Colton asked him to fill the tank and then asked if the man knew the way to the Schnooks' residence.

The man had started toward the door when Colton asked for gas but turned back when the heard the other question. He gave a long, low whistle. "Now, that's a tall order," the man said. He smiled. "Which Schnook you want?"

"How many are there?" Colton asked.

"A whole holler full," the man replied. "They own the whole holler, too. You ain't planning on driving that thing up there, are ye?" He motioned toward the rental car.

"Well, yes," Colton admitted.

The man laughed, a spontaneous guffaw that filled the small room. "Won't do it," he said, shaking his head. "You'll have a good walk from the road."

Colton liked this less and less but was determined to find Maude Schnook. He *had* to find her. He wanted to prove that Tom was still alive.

"Now, which Schnook was that ye be looking for?" the man asked.

"Maude Schnook," Colton replied.

"Maude," the man exclaimed. "She ain't been back long to home now."

Colton now could understand the language. "I know," he agreed. "She moved here from Midland, Arkansas. She and her boy."

"Well, now, since you already seem to know her, I don't mind pointing ye in the right direction to their place. It's the old home place. Knew that's where she'd end up. That Tom of her'n—" The man fell silent, shaking his head, reluctant to say more to a stranger. "I'll get that gas for ye," he said, heading toward the front door.

Colton followed, but all he could get out of the man was directions to Schnook Hollow, as he called it. As Colton pulled away from the pumps, he saw in the rearview mirror that the man was still standing there watching him.

Branch Hollow was only a wide spot on the highway, and he drove slowly through it. He watched for the "Bowers farm" the man had described to him. A quarter mile past that he was supposed to pull over at the low-water bridge. The man said recent rains would probably have the low water bridge flooded and he had warned against driving through it. But he had said there was a hand bridge where Colton could cross and then walk the rest of the way into the hollow.

Colton knew enough to realize that a hollow was simply a valley, probably a very narrow one, but still a valley. The man was right. There was water over the road. Colton backed into a wide area on the side of the road. He hoped no other vehicle came along to sideswipe him. He stopped at the walking bridge. There were no handrails. Nothing to hang on to. Boards with large gaps between them were fastened to large tree trunks with rope. True, the knots looked like they were well engineered, but Colton had not been on anything like this before. This bridge spanned a wide creek about twenty to twenty-five feet deep. Although the water standing over the road had been still, below here it was rushing over rocks in the bed of the creek.

As a boy, he would have jumped up on this bridge and ran across, excited at the danger of it all. But now, as a grown man, his fears of losing his balance and falling made him hesitate.

Coward, he told himself.

He tentatively put one foot in front of the other until he had successfully navigated the bridge to the other side. He started up a hill on a well-worn path.

Either they don't have many vehicles, or the road stays flooded a lot, he thought.

He was hot and sweaty by the time he reached the top of the hill although it was the latter part of September. It had been more of an incline that it looked.

At the top of the hill he saw the first house a short distance away. As he stepped into the clearing that served as a yard he called out.

"Hello, the house," he called as loudly as he could. In a few seconds, he repeated the call.

A large hound dog appeared around the far corner of the house. It stopped by the front steps and barked at him. It did not wag its tail, so he knew not to go any closer unless the owner came out. But if no one was home here, how could he get by this dog to the next place?

At that moment, the front door opened and a woman in a shapeless dark dress stepped out onto the porch. Colton knew he was being watched from another point in the house, probably with a gun trained on him.

"Hello, ma'am," he began. He still did not move.

"Mornin'," she returned. She would not volunteer any more words. He was the stranger, and it was up to him to tell what he wanted.

"I'm sorry to bother you, but I'm looking for Maude Schnook's place. Fellow at the service station said I could find it up this way. Am I going in the right direction?"

She silently pointed up the valley. "Third place. She's to home right now. Don't mind the blue-tick. He won't bite."

As she turned to go back inside, she spoke sharply to the dog, and it turned and disappeared out of sight around the house.

"Much obliged, ma'am," Colton called after her. He wasn't sure if she heard him or not. He laughed to himself. *Here I go again. As soon as I get around these hill people, I start talking like them. Must be my upbringing.*

He realized a simple road next to the woods went past this first house into the valley. He thought it must go past very one until the last one. As he came around a bend, he approached the second house.

He wasn't sure he would call it a house. Cabin would better describe it. And what some people called a cabin in the Rockies would be a mansion compared to this. But at least there was no dog to challenge his passing.

The road took him up a knoll. At the top, he looked down where the valley widened considerably. The middle of the valley had been cleared, and wooden zigzag-type fences delineated property lines.

He was glued to the spot. He just knew he had stepped into the scene of a documentary he had seen recently about this part of the country. A crude board house perched on the side of a hill.

Again, he was amazed at how they built their homes that way. Under the front porch was a room that was undoubtedly the kitchen. Why not build the house out in the open part of the valley? What was the reason behind building like this? He realized that question would never be answered for him.

But the scenes and the homes in the documentary were from the 1930s and 1940s, not from modern times. He didn't know there were still places like this. Hadn't he seen what he thought was an outhouse behind the second house? And wasn't this a well in this yard, fully equipped with drawing wheel and rope tied to a bucket to be lowered into the well and a full bucket of water brought up? Wasn't that a dipper hanging there? A dipper that would be used for communal drinking, no doubt.

A dog came around the building and started barking at him. A blue-tick. Although he sounded like he was going to attack, Colton knew he could believe the woman at the first house.

He greeted the house as he had before and waited patiently for someone to come.

A woman stepped out onto the front porch and walked to the railing. From her position, she was looking down at him.

As before, she waited to see what he wanted. He was consciously aware that other persons had stepped out on the porches of the two houses across the way and the next house up the valley. Word had already spread that a stranger was in the hollow and they would all be curious. They would also turn out like this as protection for each other. One man on the next porch had a shotgun under his arm. True, it was pointing down, but Colton had no doubt it could straighten and be firing before he could blink an eye.

"Howdy, ma'am," he said again to his woman. "I'm looking for Maude Schnook. The woman in the first house said I could find her here." He made sure his voice was loud enough that it carried to the other houses. He wanted everyone to know he was harmless.

"What you need her for?" the woman asked.

"My name is Colton," he began. "Six years ago, I met her husband, Tom, while I helped solve some murders in Midland, Arkansas."

As he spoke, he watched the woman's face. He had a feeling when she stepped out onto the porch that this was Maude Schnook. Now he was sure as he saw her eyes grow wide when he identified himself. They grew wide with recognition, but there was also something else there. Fear? Why should she be afraid of him?

"I'm Maude. What do you want?"

"I'm looking for Tom," was all he said. No use trying to fool her. He would get more information by being straightforward.

She was silent for a few seconds. "Why?"

Now it was Colton's turn to fall silent. He realized suddenly that he had traveled all this way, through Arkansas and now here to West Virginia, to find out if Tom were alive, to test and prove his theory that Tom was after him. But what could he say to this woman? How could he just blurt out that he thought Tom was murdering people, had made a drug addict out of his daughter and was trying to kill him? Really. What could he say?

As if the woman knew his dilemma or could read his mind, she spoke before he could answer. "He ain't here. He's gone."

Colton finally found some words. "Do you mean he's passed away, gone hunting, gone to town, or what?" he asked her.

"Just gone," she answered again, simply. She turned to go back into the house.

He knew he wouldn't get any more from her.

Because he had been looking straight up at her, he had not noticed another woman had come to the door of the room under the porch. Now he became aware of her. He looked her straight in the face, just as she was looking at him.

"She won't tell you no more," this woman said. "Best jist go back where you came from."

"But—" Colton began.

This woman also had turned back into the room. He stood there for a few more seconds then looked around at the other houses. The people were still on their porches. Although they would not have heard what Maude said to him, they knew that she had finished the business between them. He knew they would not go back inside until he moved away, back the way he had come.

A sudden feeling of defeat fell over him. He hung his head. Then he shook it and turned to go back the way he had come. He walked slower this time.

Nothing.

He knew nothing more than he did in Denver. He had driven over and around these precarious mountains and walked through the woods to this valley just to have to admit failure.

He knew nothing more than he did before.

But Tom being "gone" did not mean he was dead. And if she did not say "dead," then he could still be right about what was happening in Denver.

He had to be right.

He was so sure of that fact. His mind was so full of thoughts of what he should do next that he did not even notice that he had crossed the hand bridge.

What could he do next?

That question haunted him all the way back to Denver.

Chapter 36

L on? Commander Mitchell here."

"Oh, hi," was the response.

"How's Nancy?"

That wasn't so unusual. The commander had checked several times on her. "She's better, thanks. She'll be able to leave as soon as you say we can. Is that why you called?"

"Well, actually, I need your help with something," Colton said.

Lon just waited.

"Can you find out from your contact if there has been anyone new on the streets pushing drugs, say within the last three months? A stranger maybe? Or even a local dealing new dope. This may be a homeless person. I just need to know if anyone different has been around."

There was a pause on the other end of the line.

"It'll cost you," was the reply.

Nothing was free. Colton should have known that. But this kid? Somehow, he had expected more. Better.

"It's not for me, you understand," Lon began. "I need it for the street."

Oh. "Sure, sure," Colton agreed. Why was he relieved? Because he knew he had seen the innate good in this young man, no matter the circumstances of why he was on the streets now. "Whatever."

They set a time and place to meet so Colton could pass Lon some money.

"You know where to reach me?"

"Yeah."

Chapter 37

Dad, you wouldn't believe what happened at school today. We were just—"

Abby stopped talking to Colton as the house phone began ringing and she made a mad dash into the living room to get it.

Marsha and Abby had returned home three days before. There had not been any more ODs for a couple of weeks now.

He watched her smile as she answered. She picked up the phone from its stand, carrying it with her, and flopped down in a recliner, one leg draped carelessly over one arm. The phone rested on her stomach. She took her free hand, ran it under her long, thick brown hair, causing her hair to fly up and over the chair back.

Colton stood in the doorway, watching her. She laughed into the phone, changing positions. She saw him standing in the doorway and waved. He signed to her that he wanted to talk to her, and she nodded her head.

As he watched her, he marveled at her and felt very grateful to have her. Six years ago, he had not even known that he had a daughter. His high school sweetheart had been pregnant when they parted, he to go to college and her to go to California to visit an aunt, or so it had seemed.

But she had gone out to her aunt to have a baby and let Colton have his freedom. Had she stayed in their small, rural hometown, word would have gotten back to him some way about the baby, and he would have known she was his.

Marsha knew he would have quit college, married her, and then worked in some job somewhere to support them. And she had been right on another score—he would have hated working in some factory in Fort Spenser, which was, more than likely, what he would have ended up doing to take care of his family.

Although he was sorry he had missed many years of being with her, of watching her take her first step or say her first word, he was just grateful to have her now. And the things that had happened in the years between could be part of a greater whole.

She was a beautiful girl. She had thick chestnut-colored hair with highlights of the auburn hair of her mother. She was a happy teenager, so she was a joy to be around.

At school, she was popular with her classmates, was a cheerleader, and involved in various clubs and extra-curricular activities.

That was why he had not had the opportunity yet to have a serious talk with her about what was going on with this killer. He was more than positive she would never believe the killer was after her or Colton, but Colton was going to approach her in some way, to impress upon her certain facts and the gravity of the situation.

She would not believe because she had completely forgotten—or at least completely repressed—the events of six years ago when she had almost lost her life. Perhaps she truly had no recollection. Colton hoped this was the case. Repressed events and emotions had a strange way of coming back to haunt a person. He didn't want this happening to Abby.

He had asked the evening before when he could talk with her. Having found out that, for once, she would not be staying after school, or returning later to some activity, he had made a point of leaving the office early and letting her know he would be home, for her to stay here until he got here.

She was a respectful child, so when he made a point of needing to talk to her, she knew he was serious about something, and she took the occasion seriously. She had stayed home after school today, waiting for him.

She had no way of knowing the phone would ring just as he appeared to talk with her. To her credit, though, she did manage to talk to whoever it was for only a few minutes.

Colton noticed her flushed cheeks and happy look as she returned to the sitting room.

"A new boyfriend?" he asked. He recognized all the signs and symptoms from the last boyfriend, who was now history.

At almost eighteen and in her senior year of high school, she was not into dating on a steady basis, but she did claim a boyfriend from time to time.

These were boys to be with while at school, talk on the phone with. Colton and Marsha also let her go to the movies or on trips to the mall with a group of her friends. So far, all had gone well.

"You should see this guy, Dad. All the girls are crazy about him. We've all been trying to make him notice us. And guess what?" She said everything in such a quick, happy rush, that Colton almost missed the fact that he had been asked a question, that he was supposed to respond to something.

"What?" he asked, smiling at her.

She had returned to the sitting room, flopped down in a chair opposite him, this time sitting sideways with both legs draped across one arm. She put her head back on the other chair arm, her hair almost touching the floor. It was just that long and beautiful.

"He likes me!" she exclaimed. "*Moi.* Of all the girls he could choose from in the eleventh grade, or any other grade, for that matter, he likes me. Can you imagine?"

"Yes, I can. You're a very pretty girl, Abby." He smiled at his daughter, at her happy, bubbly spirit.

"Oh, you're my dad. Of course, *you* would think that. You're supposed to, even." She grinned at him impishly. "There's an unwritten law, or something somewhere, isn't there? But what about Amy or Trisha, just to name two others."

"Yes, I'll have to agree they are pretty," Colton said. He brought the image of the two girls to mind. They were both picture perfect, cheerleaders, popular. "But each person is attracted to something different. He obviously seems something special in you, that's all. Something that he's especially drawn to."

"Oh, Dad, he has beautiful eyes, a wonderful smile, and teeth to die for. They are so straight and white. He's just a hunk. He's just almost too good to be true."

She sighed.

Colton laughed. He was happy his daughter was happy. He had gone through this before, with each new boyfriend. She was just a normal seventeen-year-old, having crush after crush. Each one at the time was the most important thing in the world.

"So why haven't I heard of this young man before now?" he asked.

"Oh, didn't I say?" she answered. "He just moved here a week ago. He's just been in school this week."

"Oh," Colton said. That explained it. "And what about this…Craig…is it? What happened to…with…him?"

Abby straightened up in her chair. She was serious. "I still hurt, Dad, and I don't mean just physically. You know?"

Colton nodded. He saw this all the time. He was just so sorry it was happening to his own daughter.

"I think one of the worst things about all this is the fact that he seems to have rejected me now, just as quickly as he wanted me in the first place. Do you know how that makes me feel, how that looks in front of all the kids at school? Of course, I've never been one to worry so much about what other people think. You and Mom taught me that, to have my own self-confidence, but it still hurts."

"I know, but you know that will take care of itself in time." He grinned. "In fact, it seems to already be taking care of itself, with this new boyfriend."

She smiled back at him. "You wanted to talk to me?"

He was still shocked by her appearance. Along with the gaunt, emaciated look the drug had left her with, her eyes were red-rimmed from so much crying. Her whole face was blotched with large red whelps.

"Oh, pumpkin," he said softly. He sat down beside her and gathered her in his arms, rocking her back and forth gently. He stroked her hair. Years ago he had stroked her mother's hair in just the same way.

"Oh, Dad, it hurts," she said.

"I know, pumpkin, I know. Withdrawal is not easy. Never has been, never will be."

She pushed away and looked up at him. "Not that," she said, her eyes filling with tears again. "I've quit wanting the candy."

"Then what?" he asked. He was right. There could be

at least a million things she could be crying about.

"It's Craig," she sobbed.

"Craig? What about him? I still want to talk to him, you know, even if you aren't seeing him now. Has he been mean to you?"

"I—you can't talk to him."

She had started to say one thing, changed it to another.

"I can't? Are you ashamed of your old man? Afraid of what I might do to him?"

"No, of course not." She looked up at him. "He's been gone about two weeks now. One day he just didn't show up for school, and no one has seen him since. The last time I saw him, he was starting to get a cold, but no one knows where he lives, not even the school. I was going to take him some of Mom's famous chicken soup."

Ah, yes, the soup that could cure anything.

"Dad, he said he loved me, and I believed him. In spite of the drugs, I believed him. Oh, it hurts!"

As she started crying again, he just held her. Why did good girls fall for bad guys? She'd get over it, but there was no use right now trying to tell her that. She wouldn't believe it. Only time was the great healer. But she wouldn't think so for a while.

She quieted.

He decided just to take the plunge. "Abby, you may be in danger."

"Me!" she asked, incredulously. "Me? How can I be in danger? I don't use drugs any more. And I certainly don't hang around in the places where they're pushed. Besides school, that is. I know who handles them, who uses, where to get them. Everyone in school knows that. And you know that I know. We've talked about this before and you know how I feel about them. So, how can this affect me now? Dad, I don't even know any girls who hang on the streets. It's just a different world, another world, and I stay out of it. You know that."

"Yes, honey, I do know. And that's why I needed to talk to you about this." He sighed. His carefully thought-out outline of what he was going to say and how he was going to say it seemed to have gone out the window.

She had a puzzled look on her face. She had never seen her dad this way before, and it was obviously starting to worry her.

He shook his head. "This won't be easy to hear, and I told you that you won't want to believe parts of it, maybe not even all of it, but you must listen, and you must believe and take what I say seriously."

"Dad, yes, I told you I would. But you're starting to scare me. What *is* it?"

"Good. I hope it does scare you. I hope it scares you enough to make you very cautious and careful of who you talk to, where you go, and what you do until this killer is caught and killed."

"Killed, Daddy?" she asked in a little girl's voice.

"It's the only way to stop him. The problem is, I don't even know how to find him, much less stop him!"

"Please!" Abby whispered.

"Sorry, pumpkin," he said.

He took another deep breath.

Begin at the beginning, that was always good.

"You know that six years ago you and your mother came into my life. Actually, she came back into my life, bringing you with her. You've understood that I never knew I had a daughter. Your mother had her reasons for not telling me, and that's all we need to know."

Abby nodded.

"You've been my life from that moment on. You and your mother, of course. What you don't know, is that we almost lost you then. And we agreed never to tell you what happened, but now we've agreed that you must be told, for your own safety."

"Told what? And how did you almost lose me? Lose me how?"

"Abby, you were kidnapped. At that time I was able to figure out where you were and rescue you."

Abby started smiling. This sounded, once again, like one of her dad's tales that she was used to hearing.

"Really?" she asked, teasingly.

"Abby, please. It was not fun and games. You were not kidnapped by a childless couple desperately wanting a child or not even kidnapped by some sex maniac or psycho, although, at first, that's what everyone thought. You see, there had been seven other eleven-year-old children who had disappeared from Midland in the nineteen years prior to the time you disappeared. It seems that one child turned up missing every three years, almost to the same date, just as regular as clockwork. Each child apparently disappeared from the same spot, and that spot was right in front of an old abandoned house. That's where we found you, in the basement of that house, completely doped up, unaware of where you were. You were unconscious. We being your Uncle Dan and myself."

"I don't remember any of this," Abby said, with a puzzled look on her face.

"No, you don't. And I've been thankful for that. I grabbed you and got out. Dan was right behind me. The man was not there when we found you, but he attacked me from the weeds as I carried you along. Dan shot him. We killed the kidnapper. You see," Colton continued, "now my guess is that his brother is here, looking for revenge. His revenge seems to be centered toward me. The spiral pattern of these killings we talked about seems to be closing in on me, and, Abby, it's probably closing in on you, as well."

"Me? Why me? I can, maybe, understand why he would be mad at you, for killing his brother. But why me? I was just an innocent victim, wasn't I?"

When he didn't answer immediately, she started to look concerned again.

"Wasn't I?" she repeated.

"Abby, your slow drug addiction and death were going to be his revenge. He's been playing with you to get back at me. And somehow Craig is involved. I haven't decided just how yet. Maybe Craig is just an innocent pusher, if a pusher can be innocent, convinced by this person to harm you. He would be innocent of the true reason to get you hooked, is what I mean."

"I don't understand," Abby said, looking bewildered. A frown formed between her eyes. "Who kidnapped all those little girls and then me?"

"And boys, too," said Colton.

She still sounded very doubtful, but Colton knew she was trying to understand, trying to believe.

"A very deformed, twisted being."

"And you were able to figure all this out and rescue me in time before it did…whatever…to me. Which brings up an interesting point. Just what exactly did he do to the other children?"

"Well…actually…he ate them. And slowly, too, over a three-year-period, evidently, so that was why the only kidnapped one every three years."

She had blanched and gagged at the thought of being eaten. Now, she had a strange look on her face. She had been prepared to hear of sexual abuse, mutilation and finally murder, but not cannibalism. There was just something about that concept that most people could not mentally handle. It just didn't seem right, for whatever moral, ethical, or religious reasons a person wanted to put on it.

"A cannibal?"

"Not really," Colton answered, hesitantly.

"Not really? What do you mean by that? They were eaten, weren't they?"

"Yes, but the point you're missing is that this thing was *not* raised as a normal human, so it was not cannibalism. It was not aware that it should not be eating another person. The other children had been, and you were going to be simply—simply food for it. Simply food for its very existence. This…deformed person…had no concept of right or wrong, no moral dilemmas to deal with."

A smile started to appear at the corners of Abby's mouth. This was now leaving the realm of reality and starting to go in another direction.

"I asked you to listen, seriously, and *believe*, Abby. Believing is the key."

"I'm trying, Dad, I really am. Go on," she urged.

It was an interesting story. And that's what it sounded like so far—a story. Abby just stared at her dad. She wasn't sure what she was hearing, so she certainly wasn't sure what she was supposed to believe.

"You know you're always able to figure out 'whodunit' when we're talking about cases. You're always talking about having 'this' feeling or 'that' feeling about something, or someone. Aren't you always right?" he asked.

Here was something she could relate to, something that perhaps would convince her to take this matter seriously. "Yes, but—" she began then stopped.

"But, what?" he probed, gently. If she were at least thinking about this, then maybe he had a chance of convincing her.

"Well, it's just that I don't see that as having any special powers or anything." She shrugged. Then she smiled at him. "But I *am* usually right, aren't I?"

"Yes, you are." He smiled in return. "Because, somehow, you just know these things."

"I did sense something wrong with Craig, but I could never figure out what."

"Not completely, of course," Colton answered. "But you did have some sort of odd feeling that something was wrong, didn't you?" When she nodded, he continued. "Abby, darling, these killings are happening because of me. The homeless deaths, Jack's death, Dan's accident, your addiction, are all because of me. The killer is here for me, ultimately, but he will take you, also, if he can, if he's able to. And this brings us to what's happening now. These ODs are not random, not accidental on the part of the victims. A strange, unknown drug has been found to be the cause of death. You remember my talking about Jack?"

She nodded. She remembered the names of all his friends and colleagues.

"He first noticed the symptoms on the second body that came in and called me immediately when he connected the appearances of all the bodies. The only break we've had so far is that one of the prostitutes did not die from her OD and still had one of the pills. It's an unknown substance. Nothing's like it—that we know of."

"But, Dad," Abby began. He lifted his head to look at her. Her tone was very serious. "Even supposing I do decide to believe this story, what do drug ODs have to do with me? You know I'm out of that now."

"It just seems to be what he's using, dear. It's the approach he's taking to get and hold my attention. I see all these deaths as him playing with me."

"And you think he'll try to get to me another way?"

"I'm sure of it," he said, nodding.

"Well, what does he look like?" she asked. "I can keep a lookout for him, be prepared."

"That's just it. We don't know what he looks like. That's why this one young lady is so important. She's seen him."

"I don't understand. What is it?" She knew there was something else he was not telling her, something he didn't want to tell her. She stared at him steadily. She wasn't going to let him out of it. Not now. Not after such an incredible story he was asking her to believe and accept. And evidently, there was even more to this tale. "Dad?" she said.

He knew what she was asking. Well, he had told her enough, anyway. He decided he might as well tell all.

"I've just gone all the way to Midland, Arkansas, then to West Virginia, trying to find out if this Tom, this brother, is really dead, or not, as Dan believed. I've done all this because I feel in my heart that he's the one doing all this." He put his head in his hands. "But I have no real proof. I have no proof and no evidence!"

"Okay." She spread her hands. "Just supposing all this is true—"

"Abby!"

"Okay, it is true. Okay?" She was getting irritated. "It's true. So what am I supposed to do with the knowledge? I take it you've told me all this for a reason."

"Of course," Colton answered. Inwardly, he gave a sigh of relief. Even if she didn't swallow all of it, at least not right now, she was going to give him a chance to say what he needed to—what all the rest of the story had been leading up to. "From this point on, you must, and I repeat, you *must* not have anything to do with any strangers. No one at all. Even though it might go against your nature, you *must* not stop to help anyone with car trouble, help with a baby, help an old lady across the street with her groceries, or *anything*. I don't care if your actions sometimes may seem strange and even callous to your friends or anyone with you, you *must* not have anything to do with a stranger. Don't even let one approach you, for any reason. Understand?"

"Yes, but—"

"And do you promise me you'll remember this, and do as I ask? Abby, your life depends on it. Whether you believe what I've told you or don't believe, you must accept my warning. Okay?"

She had never seen or heard her dad being so serious before. "Sure, Dad. No strangers," she agreed.

"Good."

He slumped, looking as if a huge weight had been removed from his shoulders, as indeed it had. He really had not known what her response might have been to all this. "You haven't been approached by any strangers lately, have you?"

The question was unexpected. Suddenly the image of a good-looking, blue-eyed young man with a beautiful, engaging smile flashed before her. So, why had she thought of Craig in response to her dad's question?

But she dismissed it. New kids enrolled in school every day. There was nothing strange about that.

"No, no strangers," she said.

She was on the way back.

It was a new beginning.

Chapter 38

The call came two days later.

"Commander?"

"Yeah, Lon."

"There's a guy been hanging around the last couple, three months. Some think he's pushing, but no one knows for sure. The guy's a ghost. One time here, another time there. Seems, though, he hasn't been seen in a couple of weeks. You know that old house that's about to fall in, about halfway down the block from Five Points?"

Colton knew it.

"Seems he holes up there. But like I said, he hasn't been seen in a couple of weeks. One guy thought his name was Greg, something like that. He didn't talk much to people."

"Greg?" Colton echoed. *Greg?* "Craig?"

"Could be. Who knows?"

"Thanks, man."

"De nada."

The phone went dead.

Greg? Craig? Could it be? Yes, he knew it. The same feeling came over him as before. This young man was the one. Colton was sure of it.

There was no proof, and no one would believe him. But he knew.

He took Pete with him. He drove slowly past the old house and parked around the corner. Pete would go around the back.

Colton wanted to go in alone because this was now a personal thing. He could admit that now, as it had been a personal thing when it started with Abby, then he had discovered that the murders were going in a spiral, leading straight to him and Abby. This was a personal thing because of what happened six years ago.

He slowly pushed open the old door of the house. It squeaked loudly. *Oh, great. Tell him you're coming.*

Shades of six years ago. A squeaking cellar door.

Colton stood a few feet inside the door and let his eyes adjust to the dimness. The place was falling down, long ago condemned. He shook his head. Places like this around town should be torn down. They just invited the homeless and druggies to use them, not to mention the four- and six-footed creatures that would breed here.

A muffled sound came from another part of the house.

Was that a cough?

He strained to listen. There it was again. Yes, definitely a cough. It was coming from somewhere in the middle of the house. He moved toward the sound. There was enough sunlight coming through the boarded up windows to allow him to see where to step. He sure didn't want to fall through to the basement below. There was a good possibility of that in spots. He took one slow, cautious step at a time, pausing after each one. After three steps, he carefully pulled out his revolver. The safety sounded as loud as a shot itself as he released it. He was taking no chances.

Another cough kept him going in the right direction.

He paused outside the door of a small room off what had once been the kitchen. There was evidence on the counter that someone had been mixing substances. Colton moved on to the other part of the house where the cough had come from.

Suddenly he jumped into the doorway, holding his gun up and pointing it around, was prepared to go either right or left.

He didn't have to.

A man lay on an old mattress in the corner of the room. A rattling cough caused his whole body to rise below a holey, tattered army blanket. The man's arms were folded across his chest as if he was already in position in a coffin. He was young but looked old. His eyes were dark pools, sunken into parchment-like skin that seemed to be stretched over a skull. His blond hair was matted and stuck up around his head.

The stench in the room was almost too much for Colton to bear. He took short, quick breaths.

But he never took his gun off the man.

It was obvious the man had been sick for a while. He had been too sick to make it to whatever he used in this place for a bathroom. The scent of feces and urine was the strong, overlaying odor he smelled. Chances were, the young man had not moved from that spot and was lying in his own feces.

Colton didn't move any closer.

"You found me," the man said, barely above a whisper.

Colton saw the man's mouth move, but the voice could have come from the walls. It was a feathery whisper, a rasp on the wind.

"I thought you might be smart enough to find me, but I was beginning to doubt."

Again, the body gave a series of hacking coughs. It

sounded like the worst flu or bronchitis Colton had ever heard.

No, worse. This was something else.

Suddenly Colton recognized this caricature of a human as Craig, the young man who'd hooked Abby. He couldn't seem to put everything together. What was wrong with this picture? "The plant. The spiral. Abby," was all Colton could say in reply. He knew the man would understand.

The gun stayed in place.

"Abby was a good touch, don't you think?" the voice asked. "No need for that. I'm dying."

He was referring to the gun which still had not lowered.

"Nightshade," Colton said. "You handled it."

"Yes, but not Nightshade," the voice denied. "Something else. Deadly. Mom had the last of it."

There was almost an element of pride in his response.

"Nightshade for Abby, too?"

"Oh, you recognized it. Yeah, only a diluted amount each time. I didn't want to kill Abby, just make you suffer. Through her," the voice whispered. "But she was a good touch, don't you think?"

Colton's jaw tightened. It was all he could do to refrain from shooting this man. "Who are you?" Colton asked. "Why me?

The body on the mattress was gripped once more in a spasm of coughing. He lowered himself back down on the filthy mattress with a sigh. "Because of my uncle, my dad," he replied, his voice even weaker.

"Your uncle? Your dad?" Colton repeated. "I don't get it. Who are they?"

Every man he had ever arrested passed in a flash through his mind. He came up blank. Who was this?

"Otis. Tom."

Did Colton hear right? The voice was so weak he wasn't sure. "Again?"

"Otis. Tom," the man repeated, forcing his voice to be stronger.

"Otis? Tom?" Colton found himself repeating again. Was all he could do, echo this man? "I don't know…wait—the only Otis I know was a man in Arkansas." He was stunned. Yet, why should he be? Hadn't he felt all along the answer was buried in the past? Hadn't he "felt" it? So, this did have something to do with the events of six years ago, after all. He had felt it but had finally denied it as irrational, a foolish theory. "I knew an Otis Ledbetter, his friend Tom. But only briefly. I really didn't even know them."

The head nodded up and down, almost imperceptibly.

Colton couldn't believe it. He didn't understand. "I still don't get it."

"Otis is still as nutty, mentally retarded, as ever. But you killed my uncle. You drove my dad crazy. He made me promise on his deathbed to track you down and have our revenge."

Our revenge? Colton thought. "You're Tom's son," he said.

The head nodded.

So, Tom's wife *had* been a Schnook, knew the power and magic of plants and herbs. Hence, the Nightshade, or derivative thereof, according to this man.

"By uncle do you mean the monster who kidnapped and ate little girls and boys for twenty years?"

"He didn't know any better."

"And what did I have to do with Tom?"

Colton was curious as to how the mind of this man worked. Dr. Sally had explained briefly how the minds of some people worked—or didn't work, however you wanted to look at it. But it was still surprising.

"When Dad found out he was a brother to the deformed man—the murderer—and Otis, he couldn't handle it. When he realized what he had been witnessing for all those years, he couldn't handle it. And he let Otis take the blame for the boys and girls disappearing, when he knew none of them had been taken by Otis. He slowly went insane and took me with him a little, I guess. But I was taught never to break promises. And I promised. Dad said if you hadn't come along, everything would have been okay. Old Man Ogden would have died without telling anyone anything, and Dad would never have known who he was. It's your fault Dad went crazy."

The long speech took its toll on the frail body. A hacking coughing fit followed. Tears ran down the young man's cheeks, falling onto the mattress.

Colton was in no mood to show mercy. "If I hadn't come along, your monster uncle would still be eating little children, including my daughter. And you've made a game of this whole thing."

Colton pulled back the hammer on the gun, steadying his aim on the figure. He had an almost uncontrollable urge to pull the trigger.

"I promised," the voice repeated. "I promised." It was said in the tone of a little boy who had been good for not breaking his word to his dad. The crying continued. "I promised."

"You're under arrest," Colton began. "You have the right to remain silent. Anything you say can and will be used against you in a court of law. You have the right—"

Colton never finished.

Craig's eyes had shut at the word "silent."

Silent he was.

Craig was dead.

Colton lowered his gun.
The revenge was complete.

Postlude

Deep in a valley in the West Virginia hills, a few miles north of Jumping Branch, a hill thwarted the way of hikers.

If anyone ever went that way.

Halfway up the hill, hidden behind scrub in an outcrop of rock, was a crevice.

Only the slimmest of adults or a child could have crawled through the opening that served as a mouth for a cave.

Deep inside, a seed had germinated, poking its tiny head through the cold soil to touch cold, pressurized air within the depths of the cave.

It lived.

With any luck, no one would ever know it was there.

End

About the Author

Mary Jane Bryan is the co-founder of Parkland Writers' Circle, Farmington, Missouri, and a member of Thrill Writers International. She is a graduate of Missouri State University (SEMO), Cape Girardeau, Missouri, with a B.S. in Business Administration/General Management. Bryan is also a graduate of Three Rivers Community College, Poplar Bluff, Missouri, with an A.A. in General Studies.

Bryan is a strong believer in women as entrepreneurs and managers, and a past creator and owner of Jane's Muppets, a past member of Toastmasters International, which is an excellent resource for creative writing and presentation, receiving critiques and advice as needed. A past resident of Ecuador, Bryan now currently resided in Farmington, Missouri, with her husband, Peter, and Cookie, the cat.